# Not a Creature
# Was Stirring?

Look for these SpineChillers™

# SPINE CHILLERS™

# Not a Creature Was Stirring?

## Fred E. Katz

**THOMAS NELSON PUBLISHERS**
Nashville • Atlanta • London • Vancouver

Published in Nashville, Tennessee, by Thomas Nelson, Inc., Publishers, and distributed in Canada by Word Communications, Ltd., Richmond, British Columbia. SpineChillers™ is a trademark of Thomas Nelson, Inc., Publishers.

Scripture quoted from the *International Children's Bible, New Century Version,* copyright © 1983, 1986, 1988 by Word Publishing, Dallas, Texas 75039. Used by permission.

Editor: Lila Empson; Copyeditor: Dimples Kellogg; Packaging: Sabra Smith.

ISBN 0–7852–7492–8

Printed in the United States of America.

1 2 3 4 5 6 — 01 00 99 98 97 96

"I can't believe it. I just can't believe it! Why me? Why now?" I yelled the whole way back from the hospital. I wasn't usually such a crybaby, and my parents didn't let me get away with self-pity often. But this was a big disappointment for me, Conner Morgan.

My folks had been invited to speak at a marriage-counseling conference and were going to take me skiing afterward. Now I couldn't go. Why did I have to break my leg?

Ever since the summer, Dad had been promising to take me skiing the week before Christmas. I love to ski. I love having the cold air blowing against my face as I hurtle down the mountainside.

Now because of the broken leg, I couldn't go.

It all happened on the last day of school before Christmas vacation. I was in the gym practicing for gymnastics. A friend and I were doing challenges. He would do something and then I would have to try it. Then I would do something and he would have to try it.

The difference is, my friend is a little better and a little more daring.

He tried a special routine on the rings. I went behind him and completely blew it.

I climbed onto the uneven bars for my challenge. I started by swinging my midsection over the low bar and circling it. I was hotdogging and I knew it. If I wanted to win the challenge, I had to do something he couldn't do.

Next I did a handstand on the high bar, then dropped into a somersault around the low one. I looked good as I went back to the high bar.

The dismount was next. I let go of the bar and did a double somersault in midair.

I looked really good. I forgot to keep my focus and instead started thinking how my friend's eyes were probably wide open in awe.

My distraction was my downfall. Literally.

I was too close to the floor as I came out of the last head-over-heels turn.

C-r-a-c-k . . .

## 2

The pain didn't take long to hit my brain. I knew right then my leg was broken. The ski trip!

When Dad and Mom got to the hospital, I grabbed Dad's arm and begged, "Don't leave me here!"

Dad looked touched. He squeezed my shoulder. "Son, we're not leaving you. The doctor said you can go home today."

"No!" I said, realizing he misunderstood. "I'm not afraid of the hospital. I mean, don't leave me at home. Can I still go on the ski trip?"

"Conner, I know you were looking forward to this trip," Mom said, "but you wouldn't enjoy watching TV in a hotel room all day. And we wouldn't be comfortable leaving you by yourself in a town we don't know. Aunt Bergen was already coming to watch the house. With you here, now she can keep an eye on you too."

"We don't think this trip is for you, Conner," Dad said. "There will be other ski trips."

"Now, how about our getting you home?" Mom said.

When we got to the house, I sat in the living room among the Christmas tree and the decorations.

I looked at the tabletop nativity scene. It had been in my mom's family since she was a little girl. Every year we carefully placed the porcelain figurines on the table and reflected on the true meaning of Christmas.

I had always felt happy at Christmas. Until now. Every time I saw Mom or Dad carrying down a suitcase, I felt as though someone punched me in the stomach.

It was going to be a great trip, and I had to miss it. But that wasn't the worst of it.

Mom was in the kitchen getting out plates for the pizza. I called out, "Mom, since I've got to stay home, then your aunt doesn't have to come and stay in the house, right?"

She dried her hands as she walked in. "Wrong. I couldn't leave you here all alone.

"I feel okay about leaving you only because I know that Aunt Bergen will be here with you."

"Mom, I don't even know her. I've never seen her, and I would rather not have a stranger around while I'm trying to heal my broken leg."

Mom gave me a big smile. My appeal hadn't worked.

She perched on the arm of my easy chair and leaned against the back.

"This is tough for you, isn't it?" she asked, slipping a strand of hair from my eyes. "I can remember missing a horse show when I was a girl because I broke my arm. Not fun. But the Great Physician took care of me then and he'll take care of you now. You won't be lonely with him at your side.

"Besides, Aunt Bergen could use a little family around during this holiday. She's out of this world, and you will have the time of your life. She used to take care of my brother and me when we were kids. We had such a crazy time; we never knew for sure what she was up to. She used to kill us," Mom told me.

Mom continued. "I've never known anyone else quite like her. She and Uncle Charlie traveled all over the world."

She turned and left. When the doorbell rang, it took me a few minutes, but I hobbled to the front door.

I turned the doorknob and expected to see Dad's happy face smiling at me from behind a bunch of suitcases.

Instead, a flash of red and white smashed into my body and sent me flying backward.

Santa Claus? His red suit and red hat pushed through the doorway, and an inflatable Santa plastered me against the wall.

From behind Santa, Dad's big hand reached out to grab me.

"Hold it, Conner. I don't want you to fall and break another bone," Dad said.

I sighed with relief, but before I could straighten up I saw a face peering out of a black hood. The body that belonged to that face grabbed me in a bear hug.

"So this is Conner. Young man, you look just like your grandfather did at this age. The spitting image!" She flipped her hood off, and I could see her straight gray hair pulled back in a bun. It was attached by a large comb decorated in tiny faces that changed expressions when she moved. Her eyes looked at me and sparkled.

"Aunt Bergen!" Mom exclaimed as she entered

the room. Aunt Bergen's arm shot out and quickly embraced Mom with a firm hug.

"Oh, my. You are all grown up. I always knew that my favorite great-niece would turn out well. And your son, Conner, is absolutely delightful," Aunt Bergen said. Her words flowed rapidly. "Now, how can I help?"

"Just knowing that you'll be here with Conner is enough," Mom said with a big smile. "Let me get you settled in the spare bedroom."

When they left, I hobbled back into the living room to keep out of everyone's way.

The evening was filled with packing and chattering. I wasn't in the mood to share in their joy. Sure, I'd been taught Colossians 1:24 and knew to "be happy in my sufferings." But I wasn't doing a very good job of it. I think everybody understood when I went to bed without saying goodnight.

By the time I was out of bed the next morning, all the luggage was waiting in the entry hall. In a few minutes we would be saying good-bye. I had always thought it would be fun to have the house to myself. But suddenly I felt very alone.

*Alone. Alone with Aunt Bergen. It doesn't seem fair. It'll be the loneliest Christmas ever.*

When the airport van arrived a few minutes later, Dad carried the luggage out to the curb.

Mom stayed back to hug me. She whispered,

"Aunt Bergen is even crazier than I remember. There is something that you need to know about her. She is—"

Dad stepped back inside and broke in right in the middle of Mom's sentence. "We'd better hurry if we're going to get to our plane in time."

"What do I need to know, Mom?" I asked, but Mom was already grabbing her gloves and running toward the door.

She said, "I'll have to tell you when I get back." She turned and went out the door, but before she stepped onto the porch she turned back to me.

She had a serious look on her face. "Watch out! Not everything is as it seems. Aunt Bergen is not quite like everyone else."

By the time I got to the door, Mom had already stepped into the van.

*What did she mean when she said that Aunt Bergen was not quite like everyone else? When she said that Aunt Bergen was 'out of this world' did she mean that Aunt Bergen is some sort of alien?*

The van exited the driveway and headed to the airport. I turned slowly on my cast and crutches to make my way into my parents' bedroom. That's where I'd be spending the next few days.

I came face-to-face with Aunt Bergen.

"I've got a glass of milk for you. A growing boy with broken bones needs one of these several times a day," she said as she smiled at me. All I could do was smile back. She put it in the bedroom and I followed her in.

"Isn't this a wonderful time of the year?" Aunt Bergen's voice danced with happiness.

"I suppose for some other kids it might be," I responded with a Scrooge voice.

"Do I hear a bit of 'Bah, humbug' in your voice? What would a kid not like about Christmas?" she asked.

"Don't get me wrong, Aunt Bergen, I like presents as much as the next guy, but that seems to be all people think about."

"You think so?" Aunt Bergen's eyes were twinkling, but I could tell she was taking me seriously. "Go on."

"Every year I see my mom work hard trying to make Christmas special for Dad and me. If she isn't at the malls shopping, she's in the kitchen cooking. I wish it were different. I wish . . ."

"Yes?" she prompted.

"I wish we'd take the food and presents to somebody who maybe can't afford to buy them," I said. I couldn't believe I was saying all this. I didn't know Aunt Bergen, but I felt I could tell her what was on my mind.

"Ah," Aunt Bergen said at last. "So Conner turned out just like his mom. Sounds like you appreciate

9

all your mother does for you, and it sounds like she still puts others first before herself.

"Do you know what your mother used to do when she was a girl? She always saved some of her Christmas toys for the little girl at church whose father was killed in a car wreck. She said she didn't like having so much when her friend had so little.

"I don't think your mother has changed much," she said with a smile. "Here it is the week before Christmas and your folks are at a marriage conference helping others when they'd really like to be here with you. I guess Christmas gifts come in all shapes and sizes. And the best ones are the gifts you give of yourself."

She chucked me on the chin. "Go ahead and drink your milk, honey. I have a feeling you're going to like this Christmas after all—broken leg or no broken leg."

She disappeared down the hall, leaving me alone with the milk and my thoughts.

I climbed into bed for a nap. Had my mother really given her brand-new Christmas toys away when she was my age? And was I being too hard on my parents for leaving me alone with Aunt Bergen? Questions ran through my mind as I drifted off to sleep.

I was deep in sleep when I heard a faint tapping at my door. I wasn't sure if it was in my dream or really happening. I knew only one way to find out.

I went to the door and listened for the tapping again. What could be there? I twisted the knob and pulled the door open. My eyes flicked up and I jumped back in terror.

A ghastly green face! I stifled a scream.

Whatever it was, it was staring right at me.

The green-faced figure stretched out its hand toward me and spoke.

"Did I scare you? I forgot that I had this green mud pack on my face. I thought you might like another glass of milk." I choked out a "thank you," and she closed the door.

As my heart started to calm down, I looked at the glass she handed me. I set the glass on the night-stand and picked up my book and flipped to the book-mark. The book was about four kids visiting California who ended up in a really bizarre carnival. I didn't want to stop reading, but a noise distracted me.

It sounded like moaning. At first I thought it was inside my room, but the more I listened, I could tell it wasn't. I had to find out where the noise was coming from and what was making it.

Things were getting strange. I was beginning to like Aunt Bergen, but I had to admit she was a little wierd. What had Mom wanted to tell me about her? Aunt

Bergen had moved into our house, and now moaning was coming from somewhere inside the walls.

I moved slowly and quietly. I opened the door and peeked into the hallway. I couldn't see anything, but I heard the moaning again. I moved down the hall toward the back of the house. The family room and kitchen were in that direction.

As I got to the kitchen, I heard the moaning again. It was louder than before. I was getting closer.

I took another step, then stopped. The moaning stopped. I moved again, and the moaning began again. I stopped. It stopped.

I decided to take another step and go around the corner in the kitchen. I could hear nothing till I stood at the top of the stairway leading to the basement. Then it started again.

Fear kept me from twisting the knob and going down the stairs. But I knew I had to open the door if I wanted to find out what was causing the moaning.

*What could be in our basement? What if Aunt Bergen really is an alien and she's already captured someone else?*

My arm stretched out away from the crutch. I couldn't let my fear stop me. I had to look. I had to know. But I was trembling from the inside out.

My hand pulled away from the knob. I wanted to turn around and get away as fast as I could. With Mom and Dad gone, though, I knew it was up to me.

*Jesus,* I prayed, *you're going to have to go with me. I'm too scared to go by myself.*

My hand stretched a second time toward the knob. I hesitated. My heart was pounding inside my chest, and I could feel it in my mouth.

I had to do it right away before I chickened out. I grabbed the doorknob and twisted.

At the very same time that I grabbed the knob, a loud pounding rang through the house.

What was going on?

Was something trying to get out?

Or was something trying to get in?

I stumbled into the hallway. The pounding was getting louder.

Whatever was doing the pounding sounded big enough to do some damage to me if I wasn't careful.

I crept closer. The banging seemed too loud to be coming from the front door, and the closet was halfway between the kitchen and the front door.

The noise had to be coming from the closet.

When I yanked the door open, something jumped at me and I fell. I tumbled backward and grabbed the lower part of the railing going up the stairs. It stopped me from smashing to the floor, but it didn't end my fall. I slid down the wall as my attacker floated slowly through the air at me.

"The inflatable Santa Claus again. This is the second time it attacked me, and the second time it won," I grumbled.

The pounding started again. That time I knew it was coming from the front door.

Pulling myself back to my feet, I grabbed my crutches. I was a little sore from the fall but was still able to equal the record-breaking speed of a turtle as I raced along the hallway to the front door.

I was ready to apologize for taking so long. I eased the front door open, and a large brown box was pressed into my face. I couldn't see anyone holding it. The box was suspended in the air.

A voice from inside the box asked, "Are you Conner Morgan?"

I was stunned. A flying box was talking to me. I answered, "What?"

The box spoke again. "Are you Conner Morgan?"

"Yes, I am. But who or what are you? How do you do that? Who sent you?" I asked in rapid-fire succession.

"Do you want it under the tree, kid?" the box questioned.

"You can do that? You can guide yourself like that?" I wondered aloud. This was the greatest thing that I had ever seen. Was it done by remote control? Who was running it?

The box pushed its way by me as I stumbled behind the door. It took me a second to regain my balance and close the door. By that time the box was floating into the living room. Then I couldn't see it anymore. A flying box is something that a person should keep an eye on.

I hobbled into the living room toward our Christmas tree with the white lights and dried flowers spread all through it. While I was distracted by the tree, an elf leaped out from behind a chair.

His green hat and green suit almost blended in with the tree. He jumped over the gifts and headed for me. I stopped and stumbled again. I was having the worst time staying on my feet.

"There it is, kid. I just need your signature right here," the elf said as I looked up at him from the floor.

"Could you please tell me what is going on?" I asked him. I guess the moaning and the surprise Santa had rattled me. I hadn't been expecting a present—or an elf.

"I work for Elf Express. We hire every little person in town to dress up as Santa's helpers to deliver gifts," he explained. "Merry Christmas, kid."

He left as quickly as he came. I heard him shut the front door behind him.

After I climbed back to my feet, I moved to examine the package. I had taken about three steps when the pounding started again. I thought it was the delivery person. He must have forgotten something.

I hobbled to the front door and pulled it open with a big smile on my face. Only it wasn't the elf.

It was a snowman.

"Argh!" I slammed the door. Too many weird things were happening.

The pounding came again, louder than ever. I peeked out the window to the side of the door. A pair of human eyes peered out from under a snow-covered stocking cap. It was one of the younger kids from our church. I didn't know him very well. He was covered with snow.

I felt really foolish when I pulled the door open again. "Sorry. I thought you were a snowman."

"A snowman?"

"Yeah. It's been a crazy morning. Sorry to slam the door in your face."

"That's okay," he said. "Everyone is sledding down the churchyard hill. I was going to ask you to join us, but it looks like you can't go. Sorry you hurt yourself."

"Thanks." He was a nice guy. I'd have liked to go sledding with him. After I told him the story of how I broke my leg, we agreed to try again next winter and wished each other a merry Christmas. Disappointment number two.

Once the door was shut, I remembered the package. I hopped to the living room and looked behind the chair. The box had my name on it.

The box was pretty big. I dragged it to the center of the room and started pulling the tape off the flaps. It popped open, and inside was another box. That one was wrapped in red and green paper that had MERRY CHRISTMAS written all over it.

A card was on top. I hoped that the card would tell who sent it. I peeled the envelope open, ripped the card out of it, and read, " MERRY CHRISTMAS FROM YOU KNOW WHO."

I didn't know who. I lifted the gift out of the box. I guessed that what was inside would give me a clue to who sent it.

I shook the box. It didn't rattle. *Maybe nothing is in the box.* There was only one way to find out. I started ripping at the wrapping paper, sending it flying everywhere.

Once I got all the paper off, I was no closer to knowing what was inside. The gift was enclosed in a white box, and that box was taped together by somebody with lots of tape and lots of time.

What could I use to cut the tape? I looked around the room. Mom's letter opener was sitting on the table next to me. What a break! I did not need to pull my cast around the rug again. I grabbed the opener and started cutting. The box top popped open.

Inside was a brightly colored metal box. It looked like one of those tins that Christmas cookies come in. Why in the world would someone send me cookies and not sign the name?

I grabbed the top and twisted it off.

The moment it came loose, the lid went flying into the air and something sprang from the box and fell into my lap.

A snake!

I pushed at it and scrambled to my feet. I slipped and crashed back down.

It was still on my lap.

After four attempts, I exhausted my energy and crumpled back to the carpet.

It fell on my face.

Staring down my nose, I saw that the "snake" was actually a weird-looking astronaut—it looked like an alien from another galaxy. Attached to its body was a note. I sat up and removed the piece of paper to read it.

Dear Conner,

We wanted to send a little something to let you know we miss you already. Aunt Bergen is something else, isn't she?

Love, Mom and Dad

I got to my feet again. After all the excitement, I needed a drink of water. As I reached the end of the hallway, I remembered why I had gone to the kitchen earlier, when all the madness had started. I heard the moaning again.

I walked as softly as I could down the hallway. I could hear more than moaning in the basement. Things were falling over and getting banged around.

What was it? I hobbled faster toward the door. Aunt Bergen was nowhere to be seen. I decided to try the door one more time. I needed to stop whatever was causing the destruction in the basement.

I twisted the knob, but before I could pull it open, the door slammed into me. I staggered back and tripped. I slid down the side of the kitchen cabinet and landed softly on the linoleum floor.

I didn't have time to recover. The creature from the basement screamed as it leaped through the doorway.

Aunt Bergen came at me with her mouth wide open. She was behind the basement door. She stumbled for a second but caught herself by grabbing the doorknob.

"Oh, my. I'm sorry, Conner. I didn't know you were there. I hope that I didn't scare you as much as you scared me," she said with another one of her big smiles.

"I heard some moaning sounds coming from the basement, and I wondered what was making them. I never heard them before. What's going on?" I asked.

I hadn't wanted to think Aunt Bergen had anything up her sleeve, but it was getting harder to deny.

"Nothing for you to worry your little head about. Let's get you back to your room, and Aunt Bergen will bring you a nice big glass of ice-cold milk," she insisted. "I thought I heard noises up here. What was it? Did someone come to the door?"

"It was a delivery person. I got a gift," I answered.

"I hope it cheers you up. Back to your room now," she said.

"Aunt Bergen, I don't want to go back to my room. I want to know what's down there. I told you who was at the front door. Now you have to let me go downstairs to see what is making all the noise," I said.

"I don't think it's a good idea for you to climb down those stairs with that cast on. I've already been down there, and it's nothing to worry about." She smiled even bigger.

I wasn't sure I believed her, but I knew she wasn't going to let me go down there. Something—or somebody—was in our basement. Something that moaned. Even if I couldn't see it then, I knew that someday she would be out of the house and I'd get down there.

So many things had happened since I broke my leg. I needed some time to think.

Aunt Bergen acted nice, but I'd experienced things that would bother any kid. I had to stay alert and keep my eyes wide open. Maybe a little prayer time would calm my nerves.

Lying in bed staring at the ceiling, I thought through the day's events. Aunt Bergen was playing Christmas music in another room. I listened to it for a long time. I couldn't let myself fall asleep. Something or someone was in my basement, moaning. I was afraid of what would happen to me.

My eyes dropped shut, but I popped them back open. I noticed something in the room that I hadn't seen before. Above the bed on the wall was a wreath made of holly. I needed to be more observant about what Mom put in the house as decorations. Then again, Aunt Bergen could have put that in the room.

I sat up to grab my Bible. It wasn't there. I must have knocked it off. I began to swing my legs out of the bed when something grabbed me from behind and pulled me hard toward the headboard. I slid across the sheets and slammed into the bedpost. The slam knocked the wind out of me.

I struggled to catch my breath so I could find out what grabbed me. Was Aunt Bergen in the room? Had the moaner gotten loose from the basement?

Whatever had grabbed me by the shoulders started to snake its way around my neck. I reached down and grabbed some of it. I felt leaves and little berries. It was holly. I looked up at the wreath above the bed. It had sprouted little branches that were creeping along the headboard. Two thick strong ones had moved around my body.

I was caught. I was going to be a permanent absentee on the middle-school roster. I didn't want it to end like this. I didn't want to leave life lying in a bed with a cast on my leg and a Christmas holly wreath choking me.

Struggling to free myself, I ripped at the branch around my neck. I pulled that part of my body free, but as I got my neck loose, the branch curled around my waist.

It pulled me hard against the headboard once again. It was starting to play rough. Unfortunately, it was already beating me. I had better come up with a better strategy than the one I had. And I had to do it quickly. The branch was twining along my head and working its way back to my neck.

The thought hit me. *When Mom cuts holly in the backyard, she uses scissors. All I need to do is get to a pair of scissors. Where does Mom keep the scissors?* Suddenly I remembered. They were in the drawer in the nightstand next to the bed. Great—they were close. All I had to do was get the scissors so I could cut myself free.

The holly grabbed and pulled me again, throwing me against the side of the bed. Perfect—I was only inches away from the nightstand. I shot my hand out and pulled the drawer open. The scissors were there. I reached for them, and the holly jerked me into the air and threw me down on the other side of the bed.

I struggled to get away. It picked me up again and tossed me next to the nightstand. I was inches away. My fingers touched the cold metal. I grabbed for the scissors. Suddenly, into the air I went one more time. I slammed hard onto the mattress.

It was time to look at my hand. Had I grabbed the scissors? I opened one eye, then the other. Yes, I had them. I could free myself.

My joy was short-lived. The branch picked me up again, and the scissors went flying from my fingers. They bounced on the bed and then back in the air.

The next bounce could carry them to the floor or back at me. I felt as if I was watching a slow-motion movie as I saw them drop toward the mattress. They hit and then sprang back up.

I watched in wide-eyed horror.

My life depended on the random falling of scissors. I wished I had paid more attention in science and geometry classes. I might have been able to predict where they were going to land.

All I could do was watch and pray.

The scissors angled in the air and fell within an inch of my hand. *Thank you, Lord.*

I picked them up and began cutting the holly. It fell away from my neck and arms. My body was loose, and I struggled to get away.

Something else grabbed my ankle.

A spooky voice called my name, "Conner, Conner."

Again, "Conner, Conner. Wake up. You're having a nightmare." It was Aunt Bergen. I must have fallen asleep. I'd been having a nightmare! My overactive imagination had worked overtime.

"Thanks, Aunt Bergen. It was a pretty scary dream. I thought I was being choked by a holly wreath.

What's crazy is that Mom doesn't have a holly wreath in this room. See?" I pointed upward.

I stopped abruptly. "Where did that come from?"

Aunt Bergen gave me a big smile. "I found it lying around and wanted to cheer up the room around you. I was hoping that it would get you into the Christmas mood," she said.

"Could you take it away?" I asked. "After my dream, that wreath gives me a funny feeling."

She reached up and pulled down the wreath from the wall, and then she slipped out of the room.

*This is all very strange.* Aunt Bergen arrived at our house, and I heard moaning in the basement. Aunt Bergen put up a wreath, and I had one of the worst nightmares of my life. Something was going on.

To get my mind off it for a while, I turned on the TV. An old version of Dickens's *A Christmas Carol* was playing. It was one of my favorite stories, so I started watching it.

When I was little, I got really scared whenever Scrooge's partner, Marley, came to visit him. The rattling and clanking of chains scared me.

Ever since seeing that movie, I get a little worried whenever I hear chains shaking. I handle it all right, but it still scares me a little. Actually, it scares me a lot.

I should have known that if ever there was a day

that chains would clank down the hallways of my house, it would be today.

In the movie, Marley had just left Scrooge. As quickly as Marley disappeared off the screen, chains started clanking somewhere in the house.

My ears sometimes deceived me, but this time they were finely tuned to the sounds. Deep in the belly of our house, the heavy links clattered along the hard basement floor. They were moving slowly.

The sounds grew in volume. The clattering chain links climbed the carpet-covered stairs. They thumped, rumbled, clanged, and bounced. I couldn't tell what was thumping louder, my heart or the chains.

My first reaction was to climb under the covers. Then I thought that was a pretty lame idea. A thin printed, flowery sheet, a fleece blanket, and a quilt wouldn't keep out a ghost that could pass through doors.

There was no place to go. The chains crashed along the stairs and into the kitchen. Who was it? Who was coming down the hall?

The links clanked and scraped along the wood hall-way floor. I could tell that they were just outside the door to my parents' bedroom. I was about to find out what lurked on the other side of the doorway.

Thump, thump, thump. The ghost pounded at the door. The door shook with each blow. I scanned the room for some type of weapon to use in my defense.

All I could see was a can of Dad's deodorant. Could a spray from that slow anything down?

The pounding started on the door again. The knob turned and the door swung open.

I yelled, "I'm ready for you."

I wasn't.

I pulled the covers over my head. The clanking continued coming toward me.

Whoever or whatever it was stopped just inches from me. I could hear the breathing, but I was too scared to look.

A hand reached out and touched me.

"Ahh! Get away from me," I yelled as I scrambled away from the hand.

A voice broke through the clanking chains. "I'm sorry. Did I do it again? I was only bringing you some milk."

It was Aunt Bergen. I yanked the covers from my head. There she was with chains from our porch swing thrown over her shoulders and dangling to the floor. She noticed that I was staring at them.

"I found these in the basement. They will work perfectly," she gleefully told me.

"Work for what?" I asked.

"That, my little nephew, is a surprise," she whispered. Aunt Bergen set the milk down on the nightstand and turned and scurried out the door.

I heard her go back to the kitchen and then into the garage.

Something was going on, and I needed to find out what it was. The first chance I got, I was going down to the basement and then out to the garage.

I sipped my milk and settled back on the pillows to finish watching the movie. The Ghost of Christmas Present had just left Scrooge when the big clock gonged.

It gonged again.

Then the grandfather clock in our living room struck. I jumped. I'd broken the clock more than three years ago when I put a baseball through it. I couldn't believe I was hearing it.

Pulling myself out of bed, I moved toward the door. I wanted to find out how the broken clock had gonged. When I reached the door, I stopped.

Aunt Bergen was talking to someone.

Who could it be? My mind raced through dozens of possibilities. Could it be the basement moaner? This was my chance to find out who it was. Aunt Bergen had finally made the mistake of having the moaner come upstairs. I had the perfect opportunity to discover her secret.

My shaking hand reached for the doorknob. It

twisted without a noise. If I opened the door slowly enough, it wouldn't creak.

If I messed up, it could mean the end of me. Aunt Bergen already tried to do me in with a holly wreath. I was pretty sure that she wouldn't stop now.

I opened the door just enough so that I could see the living room. The voices were coming from there. I recognized Aunt Bergen's voice, but the other one sounded weird. I thought it could be a kid at first. Then it sounded more like a cartoon character. I couldn't see who was talking.

Did I really want to see who it was?

Yes, I had to know. I moved the door another inch, but still could see nothing. I opened it another inch, and I saw a small hand resting on the chair across the room from my doorway.

Fear was growing in my stomach. I closed my eyes and opened the door wider.

I opened my eyes and looked out.

I was looking straight into the wooden face of a dummy. I wasn't sure if he saw me or not. Then his left eye dropped and opened.

He winked at me.

# 11

I stared for a minute. The dummy was dressed in a matching blue jacket and pants with a red bow tie and white sneakers. His wooden head was topped by a bunch of spiky red hair.

Where had he come from? I had never seen him before. Had he been in our basement? Was he the mysterious moaner?

Aunt Bergen spoke to him, "Boris, are you enjoying your stay with my nephew?"

"Sure. He is the first kid I met who had two wooden legs like I do," Boris answered.

"Those are crutches," she said.

"Whatever you need to get you through," he remarked. "Hey, Bergen the Bedazzling, when am I going to do my little specialty for the boy?"

"I don't want anyone to see it until they are all together," she answered. "Besides, you are such a cutup. You will kill them."

I gulped. What did she mean? He was a *cutup*. He

would *kill* us. I was staring at Boris while he talked to Aunt Bergen. She answered him and then asked him a question. They seemed to be doing a comedy routine. This was all too much.

A really odd relative was watching our house and me. She had a moaner in our basement, clanking chains in the garage, and a talking dummy in our living room.

Something was definitely not right about Aunt Bergen.

*Is she an alien from another planet?* She didn't act like anybody else I knew.

I closed the door and hoped that Boris hadn't already seen me. If I was going to catch Aunt Bergen and Boris or find out about the moaner from the basement, I had to have the element of surprise.

I would yank the door open and yell, "Aha!" I had a plan, but did I have the guts to do it?

I was close to catching Aunt Bergen in her bizarre activities. All I needed was the courage. I sucked in a deep breath and reached for the doorknob again. I yanked the door open as fast as I could.

"Ah—Aunt Bergen! What are you doing there?" I gasped.

Aunt Bergen was standing smack on the other side of the door. "You scared me. I didn't expect you there."

"I was bringing you a nice glass of milk. Growing boys need lots of milk," she said with a big smile.

"You just brought me a glass," I told her.

"You're right. Did you know that two things go right away when you get older, Conner?" she asked with a hint of a smile.

"No. I didn't know that," I said to humor her.

"The first one is your memory and the second one is . . . I forget what the second one is." Aunt Bergen told her joke and broke out in a big laugh.

I nodded. My mind was thinking about something else. I wanted to get into the living room to see Boris.

"Go ahead and set it on the nightstand next to the bed. I think I'm going to sit in the living room a while," I told her as I tried to peek over her shoulder.

"I think it would be best if you stayed in bed. All that pressure on your leg from walking may hurt it," she said.

I knew she was trying to keep me out of the living room.

"I've been thinking, Aunt Bergen. Maybe you are right. I need to get back the Christmas spirit. I was thinking that if I sat in the living room around the tree, the ornaments, the dum—, I mean, the gifts, then I would catch the Christmas spirit," I said.

She bought my excuse and moved out of the way.

She let me go into the living room far too easily. A quick look around told me that Boris was no longer on the chair. Where had he gone? Was Aunt Bergen willing to let me go in there because her dummy friend was waiting to jump me? I had to be careful.

Pausing a few steps into the living room, I looked behind both walls by the doorway. He wasn't there. I took a few more steps and looked behind the chair. He wasn't there.

Just as I was about to swing my body the other way, something grabbed me from behind.

# 12

"Has it helped?" Aunt Bergen said as she touched my shoulder.

"Ahh!" I screamed.

"It looks like I've done it again," she said remorsefully.

"Done what?" I asked.

"Scared you again. It seems I'm always doing that. It's just that there are not many around where I live," she confessed.

"Many *what* around where you live?" I asked. I wanted to know because that might give me a few hints about what was going on.

"There aren't many people around where I live," she answered.

"What's around where you live?"

"You know, little things. Some are quite ancient. Some of them are quite unusual. Well, I need to get some chores done," she said as her face saddened.

39

She turned and left. Aunt Bergen didn't want to answer any more questions.

I turned to start searching for Boris again. Could he have gotten up and walked away while I was talking to Aunt Bergen?

I turned toward the Christmas tree. That's when I noticed the new ornaments on it. In all the years Mom and Dad had put up the tree I'd never seen anything like them.

They were deep red, deep blue, and deep green. Each one was made of glass or crystal. As I got closer to them, I noticed that something was inside each one. Some had Christmas scenes from what looked like English villages.

Some had faces. They looked three-dimensional. I was staring at one of the faces because it looked familiar. The face inside the glass ball was mine! I reached out to touch it. The glass ball moved slightly, and the Christmas ornament face smiled at me. I pulled back my hand. Did I really see that?

My head, minus my body and shrunk to a very small size, was inside the ornament. What was Aunt Bergen planning to do? Shrink my head? Then I remembered the comb with the faces that she was wearing in her hair when she arrived. Each face must be a trophy for her.

The thoughts had no more than popped into my mind when I heard a horrible crash in the garage. I headed toward the door leading to the garage.

I was inches away from the door when it swung open. I was afraid—but determined—to know what was there. I held my breath.

The familiar voice of Aunt Bergen said, "Don't worry about the noise, Conner. I've already been out there to check.

"You should be happy to know that only a box fell. Nothing broke. You can go back to your room now. And don't forget to drink your milk. I'm supposed to take care of you," she told me.

I wasn't going to believe that story about a box falling. Anyway, a box of what? It had sounded like a box of horseshoes falling—not like anything we kept in the garage.

I needed to get help.

In the bedroom I picked up the phone and called my friend Glen across the street. "Can you come over for a while? Aunt Bergen is really weird. I think she's some kind of alien," I said.

Glen hesitated and then said, "I really want to, but my mom wants me and my little sister to stay together while she does some Christmas shopping. If I come over Eddie will have to come too. Is that okay?"

"The more, the better. Aunt Bergen can't get us all. One of us needs to live to tell the story. See you in a few minutes," I told him. I hung up the phone and started toward the front door.

In the hallway, I almost bumped into Aunt Bergen.

I told her that a couple of kids were coming over to keep me company.

"That is so nice. You children are very sweet these days. I could just eat all of you up," she said.

"I'll bet that's exactly what you would like to do," I mumbled.

"What was that, honey?" she asked.

"Nothing, Aunt Bergen. My friends should be here any minute." I had just turned the corner by the front door when the bell rang.

Glen has always been my number one best friend. He is my exact age—we were born on the same day only hours apart. The only difference was that I was born in the east and he was born out west. We've been in the same class and attended the same church since kindergarten.

I pulled the door open and was happy to see his freckled face and skinny body.

His sister, Eddie, was with him. She's two years younger than we are and isn't afraid of anything. I was glad she was there to help.

"What's this about your aunt trying to trim down her Christmas list by eliminating one nephew?" Glen asked.

"Shh. She is right upstairs. I'll bet she is listening to everything we're saying, and you may be the next one she takes care of," I warned.

"What's happening around here? You sound totally scared," Eddie whispered.

I hobbled toward the bedroom door and said to Glen and Eddie, "Follow me. As soon as she's gone, I'll—"

"As soon as I'm gone, what will you do?"

Aunt Bergen was standing in the bedroom doorway.

"Aunt Bergen! I didn't expect you to be there. You scared me," I said.

"What do you have planned for when I'm gone?" she asked again.

"I want to wrap your gift, and I don't want you to see it," I said quickly. That was true. I did have a gift for her that I needed to wrap. Of course, I wasn't sure if I would get to it right away because there was some investigating to do first.

Aunt Bergen smiled at us all as she put on her coat. "You must be Glen and you are most certainly Eddie. Thank you for keeping Conner company while I go out. I don't think that I'll be gone long. Bye, kids. Be good," she told us.

The moment the door shut I led Glen and Eddie to the garage door. I wanted to see what had made the big noise out there. Eddie was about six steps ahead of us. She was giving us a rundown of what she thought awaited us on the other side of the garage door.

"I heard a story once about somebody getting stuffed into a chimney. Let's look there first."

Glen and I followed her over to the chimney.

Eddie hesitated and then stuck her head under the chimney opening.

Eddie immediately pulled back, ran to the couch, and buried her face in a pillow.

Glen and I were puzzled. "Well?"

"Someone is up there. I could see the bottoms of two shoes."

Glen walked across the room to the fireplace, bent over, and looked up. He pulled his head out quickly and spun around, dropping to a sitting position on the floor. He looked as if he had seen a ghost.

"What is it, Glen?" I pressed.

"Someone is up there, just like Eddie said. You can see the bottoms of the shoes." Glen looked at me. "You better take a look." He rolled away from the fireplace.

I took a little longer than usual to hobble over. I wasn't sure whether I was facing a brother and sister pulling a joke on me or whether someone really was in my chimney.

I bent over and stuck my head inside the fireplace. I closed my eyes and waited for the two of them to start laughing. They didn't laugh. They waited.

My mouth flew open the instant I opened my eyes. It wasn't a joke. Someone was stuck in our fireplace chimney.

I pulled out to face the two of them. "What do we do now?"

"Call the fire department to get the person out of there," Eddie insisted.

"Should I call the police?" I wondered aloud.

"No, don't do that!" Glen jumped in. "If you call the police and tell them that you think Aunt Bergen is an alien, they will lock you up. I'll bet she could even hide that thing up there before the cops got here. Don't say anything until you have more proof."

"Should we get him out of there?" I asked.

"I think we should try," Eddie answered.

Glen scratched his chin and then rubbed his temples. He was thinking. I waited for his smile because that would tell me that Glen finally had an idea.

Glen smiled and said, "The only thing we can do is grab his legs and pull him out."

It was a simple plan. Glen and Eddie stuck their heads back inside the chimney and each grabbed a foot and pulled lightly. Instantly, the two feet headed toward them. One shoe struck Eddie on the nose, and the other one hit Glen's lower lip.

I started to laugh. "Santa Claus was in the chimney!" I pointed as I said it and laughed even harder.

Glen and Eddie spun their bodies around only to find that the two feet were wearing black boots with red pants tucked into them.

"It is a decoration, but I have never seen it before," I confessed.

"You've seen it now," Glen said. "It looks like Aunt Bergen has struck again. It makes me think that all we'll find in the garage are more decorations of the season."

"Let's find out," Eddie said as she led the two of us to the garage door.

I took a deep breath. I didn't think we would find decorations out there. There would be more serious items in the garage.

We pushed the door open and passed from the family room into the garage. It was very dark inside.

The light switch was one step to the right. I swung one crutch that way, twisted my body, and then moved the other crutch.

I reached for the switch but lost my balance. Glen jumped over to help.

A bloodcurdling scream ripped through the darkness.

I spun my upper body, but I couldn't move my legs as quickly. I tumbled and landed on a pile of rags. Glen rolled around on the floor. Something had him.

I tried to pull myself up, but my cast kept me from doing it with much speed. I had to watch as my friend was being attacked in my garage. I kept thinking, *Where is Eddie? Did that thing already get her? Jesus, this is all my fault. They were just trying to help—please rescue them!*

My prayer was soon answered. I could hear Eddie. She was only inches from me. Muffled noises seemed to be coming from her. I thought they were muffled cries of fear.

I was wrong. She was laughing.

"I'm sorry." She giggled. "It was only a stuffed animal that bounced off the shelf when the door was opened. If there really was an alien life-form in here, we'd all be middle-school stew by now."

She stepped over to reach the light switch. She flipped it on. Nothing happened.

"Conner, the light didn't come on," she said.

"It must be turned off at the pull chain."

"No problem," Glen said. We still had enough light coming in from the family room for him to see it. Glen walked toward the light, and I got back on my feet. As he reached for the chain, something blew the door to the family room shut.

The garage went dark. Too dark to see anything.

Glen leaped into the air trying to grasp the pull chain. We couldn't see him, but we could hear his sneakers smack the concrete floor.

The chain swung back and forth against the light-bulb making a tinkling sound each time it hit. After the seventh time Glen caught it. He yelled, "All right!"

But only a dim blue light filled the garage.

"Nice light," Eddie said.

"We usually have a good bulb in there. Aunt Bergen must have changed it to that blue one," I answered. The new bulb did not give enough light. It was enough to see a little bit but not enough to see everything clearly.

The garage was filled with unusual large shapes covered by black cloths.

**15**

"It feels weird here. Let's get out," Glen said.

"Not me," Eddie said. "I want to see everything that's under these mysterious black covers." She moved to one of the shapes.

"Don't touch it!" I warned, but Eddie had already pulled on it. The cloth tumbled away from the shape. Something metal reflected the light and then flew into the air.

I watched as a sword aimed itself right at me. Glen dived under Dad's tool bench, and Eddie jumped under another dark-clothed shape.

The sword was headed for my body. How could a sword lunge by itself? Could Aunt Bergen turn herself invisible and throw a sword at an innocent kid?

I didn't have time to find out. The sword was about to hit me. I took a step backward and got tangled. My guardian angel must have been watching out for me. I tripped and fell back on the garage floor. It hurt but not as bad as the sword would have.

Eddie walked over to me. She had a funny look on her face.

"We've been fooled again. That sword was the kind that collapses. If you ask me, this whole place is a trap. What could Aunt Bergen be up to? If she's not an alien or a maniac, who is she? Or should I say, *What* is she?" Eddie went on.

Just then we both heard a muffled cry for help. Glen!

"It sounds like his voice coming from over there inside that black cloth," I said.

"Quick, we've got to find him."

"Don't worry. We'll find him," I said, but I wasn't so sure. Everything was as weird in the garage as it was in the house.

We pulled back the curtain. Nothing. His voice sounded like it was inside the back wall of the box.

"Are you in there, Glen?" Eddie called out.

We could barely hear him, but Glen's voice trailed out of the back wall. "Help! Get me out, please."

"We're trying," I told him. As I turned back to Eddie, I pulled the curtain closed. "What do we do now, Eddie?" I asked.

"Maybe we can cut a doorway into this with a saw," Eddie suggested. She pulled the curtain back to see what kind of saw we needed. When the curtain opened, Glen was standing in front of us.

Eddie and I stood there with our mouths wide

open. We were so shocked that we let the curtain fall closed again.

"He's there," Eddie yelled.

"Let's get him out of the box," I said.

I pulled the curtain open one more time.

Glen was gone again.

"Conner, where did he go?" Eddie asked. The panic was back in her voice. "We've got to get that saw so we can cut him out of there."

Eddie let the curtain close again as she started across the garage.

I wanted to take another look, so I pulled the curtain open another time. "Eddie, Glen is back. Forget the saw," I called to her. I grabbed Glen's arm and pulled him out of the box.

Glen smiled at us. "I'm glad to be out of there. Every time you closed the curtain the fake wall in the back spun around. I'm glad you figured that out, or I would have been in there a long time," he said.

"Listen, now that we're all free, we need to clean up this mess and put the sword and stuff back where we found them. Aunt Bergen could be home any minute now."

Eddie tapped me on the shoulder. "What is this?" she asked as she grabbed the corner of a black piece of cloth.

"Don't pull that!" I yelled. I didn't know what would happen. But by then I was convinced that Aunt Bergen could do strange things, and I was wary of her collection of strange contraptions.

"Look at the stuff in here. Aunt Bergen is serious about what she is going to do," I stated.

Glen looked at me and asked, "What can we do?"

"Help me get everything back in the right places so that Aunt Bergen won't find out that we've been here," I answered.

We were grabbing the things that had fallen out from under the coverings and putting them back in their original positions when Eddie called out, "Does the sword go under this cover?"

I didn't even look. I should have. She was pulling the black veil away from something we had not seen before. It certainly was not where the sword had been hidden.

As Eddie lifted the corner of the cloth and peeled it back, something crashed against the side of the box underneath the cover.

"Ahh! What is that?"

Glen and I dropped what we were doing and ran to see what she was yelling about. "What did you see?" Glen asked.

"I don't really know. I pulled the corner up, and something smashed against this side of the box underneath it. The crashing sound scared me, and I dropped the cover back on the box," she answered.

"It's probably nothing," I said.

"Then let's lift off the cover and see what is under it," Glen suggested.

"All right," I said as I boldly lifted the black cloth.

The cover slid back across a black box. The box had holes drilled all along the sides and the top.

The moment the light hit the box, something charged the side near me and banged into it hard. The box rocked, and I started tipping over backward when Glen caught me.

Glen said, "Let's just cover it back up and get out of here."

"Good idea," I said. We all grabbed corners and moved the black cloth from the floor to the air. We were ready to drop it on the box when suddenly whatever was inside slammed itself against the top. We watched the top bow out and stretch the nail holding it shut.

The box's occupant smashed again, but this time it let out a loud roar. My heart was in my mouth as the creature rammed against the box again. The top bowed and creaked.

"This box won't take another attack like that. You two should get out of here while I slow it down," I told Glen and Eddie.

Neither one argued with me. They were running for the door when the creature smashed against the side of the box.

The sudden smashing noise startled Eddie, and

55

her feet flew into the air and her back smacked the hard floor. Glen flipped over her and landed directly on top of the box as the creature crashed its body against the lid.

Glen looked up, and I saw the fear in his eyes.

A long, pointy claw was snaking its way out of one of the holes.

Eddie couldn't scramble to her feet. She lay groaning a few feet from the box. Glen was on top of the creature's box, screaming his head off. We were in bad shape.

The claw poked out of another hole only inches from Glen's face. Glen screamed again. I had to do something.

Using the crutches like gymnastic rings, I started swinging my body until I was high enough to land on top of the box with Glen. I hit the top hard, and the creature crashed against the sides.

I grabbed Glen and pushed him to the edge of the box and then off. He dropped to the floor. He was safe.

Eddie was stirring. I looked her way as she stood up. The moment she saw Glen next to the box and me on top of it, she reacted.

Eddie ran to Glen and pushed him out of the way just as the creature struck the box again.

"Eddie, Glen, I'm going to roll off the side where my crutches are. You've got to help me."

I grabbed the end of the cover that was still on the box and pulled it toward me. Then I rolled to the edge and dropped off the side to the floor below. That hurt worse than breaking my leg.

Eddie helped to pull me up and shoved my crutches under my arms. Glen grabbed the cover and pulled it over the box. As soon as he did that, the growls and ramming ceased.

"I think it's over," I whispered.

"Let's get out of here," Eddie whispered back.

"I have to put the sword away first." I did that while they ran toward the door and opened it so I could swing the big cast in ahead of me.

"The light," I yelled. "We've got to turn out the light!"

Eddie's hand slipped inside the door and flipped off the light. Whew! We were safe in the family room. No more creatures in dark, black boxes. I hoped that we got everything back in the right places.

Just then we heard moans coming from the basement.

"Is that the sound you told us about?" Glen asked.

"Yes. What does it sound like to you?" I asked, hoping that he would have an answer. But I wasn't ready for the one I got.

"I once heard the same sounds in a horror movie," he answered. "Do you remember, Eddie?"

"Yes, but those moans don't sound like what I heard. Conner, why don't we just open the door?"

"I want to," I told her. "But look what happened in the garage. I don't want to take another chance like that."

Glen reached for the knob.

"I have the feeling that Aunt Bergen is hiding something," I told him.

"It's probably nothing at all," Glen said quickly.

"Or it could be some alien plot to trick you into going to the basement," Eddie added.

"I've got to do it," I told them. I reached out and twisted the knob.

"Conner!"

I jumped. Aunt Bergen was home! We couldn't let her know that we were even near the basement door.

"Quick, sit down. Let's act like we came out here to have something to eat."

I shoved Glen and Eddie toward the kitchen table with one hand and grabbed some Christmas cookies that I saw on the counter with the other hand.

Aunt Bergen entered the room with an armful of bags. She looked our way, dropped her bags . . . and hurled herself at us.

**18**

"Don't eat that!" she yelled as she ripped the cookie from my hand. Glen and Eddie dropped theirs before mine hit the table.

"Aunt Bergen," I said with surprise. "Why did you do that?"

Maybe she had put poison in the cookies and didn't want Glen and his sister to eat them. Maybe she was saving them for the rest of my family when they got back. First me, then them.

Aunt Bergen said, "Honey, I made those for Christmas tree decorations. They would taste terrible."

I didn't believe her, but I had to admit that she came up with that idea quickly. Glen and Eddie were staring at us both.

Glen spoke up, "I think we better go now."

He and Eddie were going to leave me just when I needed them to stay close. "You don't have to go yet. We could play a game or something," I told them.

"No, we probably should get home before Mom calls to see if we are still alive," Glen said.

"We'll call you later to see if you are," he added.

"Alive?" I asked.

"That's what I mean," he said.

Glen and Eddie headed toward the front door. I felt as though I was watching the crew leaving a sinking ship.

I decided to follow them to the front door and then to slip back into my parents' bedroom in the hope that Aunt Bergen wouldn't get me there.

I didn't hear her footsteps behind me as I settled onto the bed. I left the door open a crack to give me a view of the hallway.

Several minutes passed before I calmed down enough to pick up my Bible and begin to read. My eyelids were drooping after about fifteen minutes. I had just closed them when I heard a scratching noise in the hallway.

At first I couldn't tell what it was, or maybe I just didn't want to believe that I was seeing what I thought I saw. A red elf cap bounced along the wall, and underneath that cap was the body of one of Santa's elves.

I didn't believe in elves or Santa Claus. But an elf was in my house.

A minute later a green-capped Santa's helper bounced by. Then a third one skipped down the hallway.

The front door closed behind each one. Aunt Bergen would walk back along the hallway and lead another one toward the door. I watched her do that until my curiosity got me out of bed. I wanted to catch her as she led a resident of the North Pole through the house.

As I moved across the thick carpet in my parents' room toward the door, I saw Aunt Bergen cross the hall heading to the kitchen. I dragged my cast, trying not to make a noise. I wanted to surprise her.

My breathing was heavy and my heart pounded hard.

If I opened the door and caught her, would she wipe me out right then?

If Aunt Bergen really was from out of this world, she could probably zap me with some kind of laser beam. I had to be careful.

I reached for the door and stopped. I said a prayer, took a deep breath, and prepared myself for the moment of truth.

Before I could open the door, something came flying at me.

Aunt Bergen's hand was racing toward me. And something was in her hand. Her words snapped me to attention.

"Conner, I thought it was time for a nice glass of milk to help those bones grow strong. Drink up," she said to me with her big smile.

"Thanks, Aunt Bergen. I was just coming out to see about all the noise in the hallway. What's going on out here?" I tried to smile so she wouldn't think that I had seen the elves.

She tousled my hair. She said, "Nothing to worry your little head about."

"I really want to know," I said emphatically.

"All right then. It was Santa's little helpers." Aunt Bergen giggled, then turned around and headed back down the hallway.

I wanted to ask another question but she was around the corner before I could say another word.

"Aunt Bergen, I need some things from my room

upstairs. I'm going up there for a few minutes," I called to her.

Her faint voice from the living room said, "That's fine, honey."

My cast wasn't easy to move up all the steps, and my lack of skill with crutches made the trip unusually difficult. I was nearly out of breath by the time I made it to the top. The hobble to my room took a long time. I was exhausted by the time I dropped onto my bed.

I managed to roll over and grab the phone. I needed to tell Glen what had just happened. I could hear Aunt Bergen moving around downstairs. That meant I had plenty of time to get hold of Glen.

The phone rang three times before Glen picked it up. "Hello."

"I just saw the strangest thing," I told him.

"That is nothing new for your house lately," he joked.

"This isn't funny," I reminded him. "I came upstairs to call you because I needed to tell someone what I saw before it's too late for me to tell anybody anything."

"Go ahead. I'll even write it down in case something happens to you," Glen said.

"I was lying in bed in my parents' room. The door was open a little, and I saw Aunt Bergen walking with a group of Santa-type elves. They headed down the hallway and out the front door. It was really weird," I told him.

Glen was quiet on the other end of the line. I could hear the scratch of pencil on paper. He really was writing it down. I guess he realized how serious my situation was becoming. Then I heard his mother's voice in the background. "I'll check with you later— I've got to go," he told me and then the phone clicked.

I hung up the phone and made my way into the hallway. I called for Aunt Bergen. No answer. She must have been in some other part of the house, far from me.

I had a chance to search her room, and I intended to take it.

But something pricked my conscience. Snooping around in someone's room was disrespectful. And I had always been taught to honor and respect my elders.

*But I've never been told to honor and respect an alien,* I rationalized. I had to go for it.

The guest bedroom wasn't very large. I wasn't sure what I might find there, and I didn't even know what to look for. What would an alien have in her bedroom? A secret decoder ring?

The door to the room was slightly open. I pushed it and said quietly, "Aunt Bergen?"

The coast was clear.

My cast and crutches made it hard to slip around smoothly and quietly, but I had to be as silent as possible. The room had a closet, a bed, and a dresser. At the foot of the bed was an old chest that Mom kept blankets in.

I went to the dresser first. I pulled open the drawers and quickly looked inside. Nothing out of the ordinary caught my attention. I finished with the drawers and started to turn away.

I noticed a picture frame lying facedown. I flipped it over. It couldn't be . . . but I was looking right at it.

Aunt Bergen was floating in the air on her back with nothing to hold her up.

A man was standing beside her with his arms in the air. I figured he had to be Uncle Charlie, her husband. Was he making her float?

That picture was enough proof for me. Normal people simply don't float in the air. I knew I couldn't keep the picture, but somebody else needed to see it. I decided to call Glen back and get him to come over again.

Before I left Aunt Bergen's room, though, I wanted to peek in the closet. That was where she would keep anything like a radio beam transmitter or any other space paraphernalia.

I pulled the closet door open. It squeaked. That made me nervous. I couldn't let Aunt Bergen catch me. If she was really something else besides my aunt, I needed time to foil her plan of taking over my family.

I gently pulled a little more on the door, but it swung open rapidly. It almost pushed me out of the way.

Something very large and dressed in a black hood pushed on the door and fell on top of me.

I stumbled backward and landed flat on my back on the bed.

The bed kept me from falling, but the bed couldn't protect me from what was attacking my face.

# 20

I struggled to get away. I punched and pulled. It stayed with me. I struggled to my feet and knocked my attacker to the floor.

Then I got a good look at it. It was only Aunt Bergen's black-hooded cape. I picked it up from the floor and walked over to the closet to see what else might give me cardiac problems.

The closet looked fairly harmless except for a suitcase that was pushed as far back in the corner as possible. That looked suspicious to me. I tried to reach it, but my cast prevented me from bending over and grabbing the handle.

I had an idea. I could use one of my crutches to hook the handle and pull it out far enough for me to grab it. I aimed the tip of the crutch and hooked the handle. I slowly dragged the suitcase in my direction until it was within my reach.

My heart was beating hard again. Inside the suitcase might be the answers to all my questions. All I needed to do was get it open before Aunt Bergen came looking for me and caught me.

I laid the suitcase on the floor and opened the latch. Just then, the phone rang.

I needed to get out of Aunt Bergen's room quickly. If the phone was for me, she would search for me and find me in her room. If it wasn't for me, who else would be calling Aunt Bergen except some other aliens?

I was afraid to chance hanging around. The suitcase would have to wait.

I shut the suitcase and slid it back into the closet. I pushed the door shut and hobbled to the hallway.

I needed to get downstairs to find out who was calling on the telephone.

On the trip back down the stairs I was very quiet. I hoped to slip into my room before she knew it. As soon as I could, I wanted to quietly pick up the phone and call Glen. I didn't want Aunt Bergen to hear me and come rushing in.

The trip down was faster than the trip up. When I arrived at the bottom, I slowly approached the room. The door was open. I could hear Aunt Bergen in the bathroom off the bedroom. She was singing "Have Yourself a Merry Little Christmas" while she cleaned.

The phone call must have been for her. Just as I had suspected—the other aliens were probably interested in Aunt Bergen's progress in taking over our family. How long until they all would invade our house?

I looked in the bedroom. There he was again. I couldn't believe it. He was sitting on the bed. I looked into his eyes, and I was sure that Boris winked at me again.

# 21

I spun around as quickly as the cast would let me. I didn't want to climb the mountain of stairs, but I needed to if I wanted to carry out my idea.

When I got to the top, I waited for a minute and then called down to her, "Aunt Bergen, I'm heading down now. If you hear a clunking noise it's just me falling."

She didn't answer.

I called again. Still no answer.

She must have finished cleaning in the bathroom while I was climbing back up the stairs and moved on to the family room.

I was too tired to walk the steps again, so I held my crutches up in one hand slid down the banister. When I hit bottom, I hopped to the bedroom expecting Boris to be sitting on the bed. He wasn't.

He was there just a few minutes earlier. *Where did he go?* I asked myself. Dummies don't get up and walk away. He had to be nearby. I was sure that if I found Aunt Bergen, I would find Boris.

I shifted my clumsy cast around and guided it into the hall.

"Aunt Bergen," I called. No sound returned.

I called again. Still nothing.

She must have stepped outside. If she had gone out, I was alone in the house, and that meant the basement was waiting for me.

The move down the hallway was quicker than usual. After so much walking around on my crutches, I was getting better at moving with one leg in a cast. I reached the basement door in no time.

I stopped to listen for Aunt Bergen. She wasn't around. My heart was thumping inside me. Even my breath came in short gasps. I murmured to myself, "Here goes nothing."

When I tilted my body to grab the doorknob, my left crutch slipped from my hand and smacked the wood door. My arm jerked toward it and caught it like an acrobat grabs a trapeze bar.

But it was too late. The noise was already echoing in the other rooms.

I cupped my ears and listened intently. Still nothing.

Then a faint sound came from the other side of the door. I heard the long nails scratching at the wood. Low moaning started soon after the scratching.

I couldn't do it. I couldn't open it. I was so scared my teeth chattered. I was paralyzed by fear.

"Perfect love takes away fear, perfect love takes

away fear," I repeated to myself hurriedly under my breath. First John 4:18 had given me courage before, and I really needed it now.

The only thing that kept me from the unknown was the basement door.

What was on the other side? Someone Aunt Bergen had captured? Even though I was scared, I had to find out. It might be my last chance. If I waited, it might be too late. Whatever Aunt Bergen had in mind for me, she wasn't going to wait forever.

My parents would be coming home soon. She needed to get me out of the way before then so she could get ready for them.

I reached out. The scratching stopped. Whoever or whatever was in the basement was waiting for me. I *had* to see what it was. I had to be brave. I grabbed the knob.

"Conner!" Aunt Bergen called from upstairs. "Conner, where did you go?"

I couldn't let her know that I was trying to get into the basement again. I looked around for a place to hide, but I couldn't see anywhere that a guy on crutches lugging around a plaster leg could squeeze into.

Then I realized there was a good place outside. The sliding glass door to the patio was only a few feet away. I could get to the door and then slip out of it.

Stumbling to the door, I slid it open. I was watching

the room behind me and didn't see the bike on the ground. I tripped over it but was lucky enough to be close to the picnic table so I could drop down on the seat.

I was smiling to myself because I had fooled Aunt Bergen when an arm and a hand draped over my shoulder.

I snapped my head around and found myself looking straight into Boris's eyes.

I scrambled to my feet and spoke softly to him, "Listen here, pal. I know what is going on around this place. The two of you are planning to eliminate my family so your alien buddies can invade our bodies.

"Well, you can just forget about it because God's Spirit, who is in me is greater than the devil, who is *out* in the world," I said, paraphrasing 1 John 4:4 slightly. "I'm on to your plan. I've already called the cops and they'll be here in a few minutes. So don't try anything funny."

Boris stared back at me and then slumped a little. His arms popped up in the air. He was surrendering.

I must be going nuts. I was threatening a dummy and getting ready to do a citizen's arrest.

What was even crazier was that the dummy was surrendering peacefully.

"Just stay right there, you termite feast. Don't come any closer!"

My words fell on deaf ears. He slid down farther

on the picnic table seat. Then he fell to his side onto the seat with his face buried in his hands.

He didn't move. I thought he was filled with sorrow and remorse. I must have been too softhearted. I changed the way I spoke to him.

"I'm sorry that I spoke so harshly to you. You have to understand that since you and Aunt Bergen moved in, my life has been filled with the most bizarre happenings. I need some answers. Are you willing to answer some questions?"

He made no movement. I pushed Boris back against the side of the picnic table. He toppled to the wood deck with a thump. His eyes closed.

*Oh, no!* If Aunt Bergen hadn't made up her mind whether to get rid of me yet, I just helped her decide. My recent action was going to cement her decision.

My name was going to be on a tombstone. She would most likely let the creature that was scratching at the basement door with its long, pointed nails have me for dinner.

If Aunt Bergen was really an alien like Glen said, she could do just about anything to me. All the possible horrors waiting for me flashed before my eyes.

Aunt Bergen's voice broke into my thoughts. It sounded like she was calling me from the front yard.

*Good!* That gave me a chance to slip back inside. The sliding glass door opened with my tug.

I peeked around the corner. No Aunt Bergen.

The front door closed just as I made my way back into the kitchen. Aunt Bergen was back inside.

"Conner!" she called.

"I'm right here, Aunt Bergen."

She entered the kitchen. She had a puzzled look in her eyes. "I've been looking all over for you," she said. "I was so worried. Could you hear me?"

"I'm sorry if I scared you," I told her with a concerned tone in my voice. I wished she was sorry she scared *me*.

"It's just that I have so many plans for Christmas Day for your family," she said. "I also thought it might be time to try some of them out on you."

She smiled. It was a smile that was used only when somebody was asking somebody else if he wanted to do something fun. I had a feeling it wasn't going to be much fun for me.

The time was getting too close. She just said she wanted to try her plans out on me first. She had to get rid of me before I had a chance to warn my parents when they got home.

My parents would be home Christmas Eve, so she was probably planning to take care of them on Christmas Day. Somehow I had to survive. I had to make it to Christmas Day in order to warn my parents.

"Exactly what are you going to try out on me?" I asked, even though I really didn't want to know.

"Well, I thought I would start with the—" She was interrupted by the phone ringing.

She hurried to the one in the living room, and I reached for the one in the kitchen. We snapped up our phones at the same time. "Hello," we echoed into the phone.

"Hi, Conner. Hi, Aunt Bergen. How are things at home?" Mom was on the line.

"Just fine, dear," Aunt Bergen said. "Conner and I are having a great time."

Mom needed to know what was in my future and in theirs. With Aunt Bergen on the other phone, I couldn't say a word. At least not a direct word.

I had an idea. Maybe I could send a message in between the lines by stressing certain words. It was worth a try. Anything was worth a try.

"I sure miss everybody, Mom," I said. "But Aunt Bergen *kills* me. Her little jokes really *choke* me up. We have done so much that I'm afraid I'm going to end up *dead*."

"That's great, Conner. Aunt Bergen, thanks so much for taking such good care of him," Mom said.

She hadn't gotten the message. My code wasn't working. I had to try harder.

I jumped in again. "She's got me running around like a chicken with its head *cut off*. Her jokes *slay* me."

"My goodness, Aunt Bergen, I've never heard

Conner so happy to have someone staying with him before. We need to have you over more often," Mom said.

She still didn't get it.

Maybe I needed to be more direct. "I sure miss everyone, Mom. When are you coming home? I'm *dying* to have you come home."

"Well, that is why I called. We got snowed in, and we are not sure if the plane is going to get out on time. We may be here for an extra day," she told us.

Panic set in. "You can't. I'll *die* if you don't get home soon." I meant it too.

"You're being a little dramatic, don't you think? You have been away at camp longer than this. We'll be home soon.

"I have to go now. I'll call to let you know when we'll be home. Your dad and I love you, honey. Bye," she said as she hung up the phone.

I put the receiver down and turned to see Aunt Bergen walking into the kitchen toward me.

She looked around until she found what she was looking for.

She reached over and picked up Mom's largest knife.

**23**

"Wait a second, Aunt Bergen. I was only kidding on the phone. I could stay here forever with you," I pleaded.

"That's nice, Conner, but one of us has to go." She smiled.

"I feel like going for a walk. I think I'll step out for a minute." I fumbled out the words. I needed an excuse that would carry me away from my aunt with the knife.

"I'm afraid that I can't let you do that," she stated sternly. Aunt Bergen took two steps toward me.

I couldn't believe that it would all be over so soon. I mumbled to myself, "This stinks. This really stinks."

"Instead of going for a walk, dear, why don't you go to your room? I'll have things ready for you in a few minutes." She smiled again as she said it.

"Things?" I blurted out. "Do you call what you're going to do *things*?"

"Don't be upset. I do it all the time. As you kids say, 'It's no big deal.' I'll come get you when everything is ready," Aunt Bergen said.

I quickly hobbled off to my parents' bedroom. I had little or no choice in the matter. Aunt Bergen— or whatever it really was—was preparing to finish her task. I was afraid that I was that *task* she had to finish.

I tried to think. Aunt Bergen could complete the job at hand in several ways. She could release whatever was moaning in the basement. She could let Boris creep into my room. Or she could carry me off herself to her spaceship.

I had to protect myself. I would build a booby trap for anyone who entered the room.

I had to work fast; I didn't have much time.

In the bathroom I found a sponge mop. I balanced the sponge mop on top of the doorknob. If my attacker opened the door, the mop would fall. It would make a noise, but it wouldn't protect me.

If the door opened, the sponge mop handle would fall to my right. I needed to put something in the path of the fall. I searched for something I could use. I noticed that the dresser was in the right position. If I placed something over its edge that was long enough, it would act like a catapult.

Hanging on a hook in the closet was a long shoehorn. I had given it to Dad last Christmas. I had no idea if he ever used it, but I could. Holding the long shoehorn in my teeth, I dragged my cast behind me as I hopped on my crutches. I carefully positioned the shoehorn on the end of the dresser. I grabbed Mom's big bath puff, drenched it with talcum powder, and placed it on the end of the shoehorn that remained on the dresser.

The falling sponge mop would strike the end of the shoehorn that hung over the edge of the dresser. The powder-filled puff would go up in the air and smack the intruder in the face. This would cause her or him—or it—to be temporarily choked and blinded so I could get away without getting caught.

My eyes scanned the room again. I wanted something on the floor that my attacker would slip on.

Nothing.

I went back to the closet and saw something that would be perfect. A silk pillowcase! Placed on the floor in front of the door, the intruder would slip when stepping on it.

Feeling fairly safe, I curled up on the bed. The day had worn me out. In a few minutes my eyes were closing. I did not realize that I had fallen asleep until I woke up and discovered the sun was down. At first, I didn't know where I was. I heard noises. I didn't know if they were part of a dream or for real.

"Conner, it's time," Aunt Bergen said from the other side of the door.

"Wh . . . what is that?" I slurred my words.

"I said it's time. I'm ready for you to come out now," she said.

"I'll be right there," I said. I flopped my legs with a thunderous clump to the floor.

My head felt like it had goo in it. I couldn't think.

I tried to shake the goo out of my head, and I was still shaking when I stepped on the silk pillowcase. I couldn't stop myself from moving with it toward the bedroom door.

But before I slammed into the door, my body crashed hard on the floor.

It was dark, and I forgot about the mop on the doorknob. I wanted to pull myself up, so I grabbed the knob. The mop flipped over, and the powdery puff smacked me in the face.

The white dust covered my hair, face, and body and blinded me. I wanted to scream, but when I sucked in air, a few bits of the white powder rushed up my nose.

It tickled. A hurricane-force sneeze was about to come. "Ah-h-h-h choo-o-o!"

The windows and the door shook and rattled.

"Are you all right, Conner?" she asked.

"Yes, I'm fine. I just tripped. I'll be out in a minute."

I tried to wipe off the powder, but it was hopeless. When I got to the kitchen, Aunt Bergen stared at me.

She lowered her eyebrows as if she was trying to think of a question.

Aunt Bergen broke out in laughter.

"You look like you have just seen a ghost. Should I get the feather duster and dust you off?" she asked.

"Oh, no. I'm fine. What do you have waiting for me?" I asked, even though I didn't want to know.

"It's something very special. I just hope that you don't get excited and run around like a chicken with its head cut off," she told me. As she finished her statement, the phone rang.

Aunt Bergen lifted the receiver. She did not say much after "hello," but when she hung up the phone, her face was beaming.

"It will have to wait. I just got a phone call, and a special surprise has come in at the bus station. I need to call a cab and get down there right away," she said. She hurried to the closet to grab her coat.

The cab was at the house in less than ten minutes.

As I watched Aunt Bergen leave, I thought to myself, *What in the world could be at the bus station? Or who? Buses usually carry people. Were the other aliens coming in by bus?* Nothing made sense.

I stood to go back to my parents' room and suddenly remembered that I could go down to the basement to see what was there. I had dragged my cast only a few steps when the doorbell rang.

I had to take care of the visitor at the front door before I could check out the basement. I headed that way, slowly pulling my extra weight with me.

The doorbell rang again. Whoever was there was impatient.

I pulled open the front door. A blast of snow blew into my face. The icy particles blinded me for an instant. Before I could wipe the snow from my face, the delivery man wished me "Merry Christmas" and started back to his truck.

It looked like a terrible storm had picked up. The wind continued blowing snow into the house.

I slammed the door.

That was too bad because I never got to see what was being done in our front yard.

The package wasn't for me, so I left it at the front door. I didn't have time to place it under the Christmas tree. I had to get to the basement door.

The walk back to the kitchen seemed to take forever. Or maybe it seemed so long because I was so very tired.

When my cast hit the linoleum floor, there was another ring. This time it was the phone. The whole world seemed to know that I was up to something very important and was determined to stop me.

I picked up the phone and said, "Hello."

"Conner, it's me, Glen."

"I know it's you. What do you want?" I fired at him.

"I was calling to see if you are still a member of the human race or have you become an alien?" he quizzed.

"That's a silly question," I said. "If I were an alien, do you think that I would tell you? You should ask me something that only I would know."

"Like what?" he asked.

"That's another silly question. If I tell you what to ask me, I would already have the answer. You need to ask a question that you know the answer to," I told him.

"I get it," he said as if a lightbulb lit up over his head. "Here's my question. What did I have for breakfast this morning?"

"Glen, the question needs to be something that both you and I know the answer to," I said. I was getting frustrated with him.

"Conner, I don't need some silly question to know it is you. Nobody but you could get all worked up about something like a question. You must be you." Glen laughed.

"Thanks for the call, Glen. I'll see you later. Right now, I've got to get down the basement stairs to see what is there," I told him as I hung up the phone.

I took the few steps toward the basement door. I would finally find out who was living underneath our house—and why.

I twisted the knob and pulled the door open.

At the same time, the front door slammed open.

Aunt Bergen yelled, "Help!"

# 25

"Come quickly, Conner. I need a little help getting this thing in the door," she called urgently.

I hobbled down the hall, watching the snow blow all around her. She was pushing a box in with her feet and trying to close the door. By the time I reached her, the door was nearly closed.

"I can't wait for you to see what is inside this box. Unfortunately, I need to save it until your parents are here," she said. She smiled again.

"You can give me a little hint, can't you?" I begged.

"Oh, I can't do that. I want it to be a big surprise for the family. But I do have a surprise waiting for you in the kitchen. Follow me, young man, for the one thing I do that people would die for," she told me.

So this was it. This was the end. I wished that I could warn my folks.

I was about to be cornered in the kitchen by Aunt Bergen.

Strange elves were lurking on the front porch.

A weird dummy was on the back porch.

A killer beast was trying to escape its box in our garage.

And a mysterious moaner was in the basement.

I had nowhere to turn.

*This is it, Lord,* I prayed. *Just you and me.*

I followed until she stood directly in front of me and held out a cloth. She said, "I want you to blindfold yourself."

My stomach was doing flips, and my mouth went dry. Aunt Bergen led. She turned me around until I was dizzy. I was thoroughly confused. I didn't know where we were in the house.

Then she stopped me.

"Are you sure that you can't see?" she asked. I nodded that I couldn't see. To tell you the truth, I was so scared that I honestly didn't want to see. "Now lean forward," she said.

I didn't know what to do. I was scared, but I couldn't run. Even if I could get to the door, the elves were waiting outside.

I was trapped.

She again encouraged me to lean forward. I drew in a breath and said another prayer.

Then it hit me.

**26**

Aunt Bergen had spent her day making me my favorite meal. I smelled the spaghetti sauce before I opened my eyes. She had made me cheese ravioli with meatballs.

"Aunt Bergen, how did you know that was my favorite?" I asked with surprise.

"Your mother left a list of things I could do to get your mind off not being able to go on the trip. This was one of them. Sit down and eat up. You never know if you'll ever have another meal again." She giggled out the words.

What did she mean by that? Was it my last meal? Was it poisoned? I really didn't want to find out, and I didn't. Aunt Bergen's head and mine spun toward the front door when we heard a loud hammering outside.

"Finally. I thought they would never get here," she said. She hurried down the hallway and out the front door.

I couldn't keep up with her even if I wanted to. I

started hobbling down the hallway to see what was going on. As I reached the front door, Aunt Bergen flung it open and walked in. Her face was brightened by a smile.

"What's all the noise?" I asked. I was puzzled.

"Some workers are finishing up some things out front," she answered.

That wasn't enough information for me.

"What things are they finishing up?" I asked.

"The kind of things that will make people want to come to your house," Aunt Bergen said, then she giggled.

I'd already figured out that she giggled only when she was preparing to eliminate someone.

I was ready to ask more, but she hurried down the hall again.

It was all getting to be too much for me. I needed my parents to come home. I didn't have a plan to save me or them, and I needed some help—some divine help.

The rest of the night I plotted how to rescue my folks from the elves hiding somewhere outside. I didn't want them—or me—to join the moaner in the basement.

Before I could come up with a good plan, I fell asleep. I was not that deep in sleep when I heard a noise from the living room. I was not sure what it was. I had never heard a sound like it before.

In the beginning, I thought I imagined it, but the

more I listened, the clearer I could hear it. The noise was joined by another noise. I knew the second noise. Someone was in the rocking chair in our dining room.

The rocking chair was one of Mom's favorite antiques. Her grandmother had given it to her. It was made out of really dark wood. The craftsperson had carved ornate scrolls all around it. The cushion had been recovered so the whole thing looked new. But Mom said it was very old. All of us kids were supposed to stay away from it.

Whoever was rocking didn't know that Mom didn't want anyone using it. I really didn't want to know who was breaking Mom's rule, but for the sake of the rocking chair and for the sake of the person breaking the law of the house, I had to find out. Most likely it was Aunt Bergen. Who else could it be?

*That's a silly question*, I thought. It could be an elf. It could be Boris. It could be any of Aunt Bergen's alien friends.

Suddenly, I realized that sneaking down the hall to see who was making the weird noise and sitting in the rocking chair might not be a great idea.

I threw my body back onto the bed and pulled the covers over my head. The noise continued along with the creaking of the rocking chair.

Above me I heard footsteps. They were Aunt Bergen's. I could track her movements upstairs by her steps.

*If she's upstairs, then who's in the rocking chair?*

I pulled my body out of the covers and the sheets. Throwing my legs over the side, I found my crutches and headed for the bedroom door.

I peered out. I wanted to make sure that Aunt Bergen wasn't standing there with a glass of milk. I had been scared by that once too often.

She wasn't there. I moved quietly into the hallway. Aunt Bergen walked around in her upstairs room. I was safe from her attacking me, but I was not safe from what sat in the rocking chair.

I made my way to the opening that led to the dining room.

The chair was on the other side of the wall I was leaning against, so I could not see much of it. A partial reflection in a mirror let me see the front of the curved wood that allowed the chair to rock.

Some kind of feet should have been moving the chair. I couldn't see any. There were no feet at all. The chair was being rocked by something invisible.

What in the world could be invisible? My breath was coming in short bursts. I was extremely frightened.

Whom was I about to come face-to-face with?

The truth instantly dawned on me. I was looking in a mirror, and I'd read that certain creatures could not be seen in a mirror. I had always laughed at such nonsense. But now I wasn't so sure. Maybe aliens couldn't be seen in a mirror either.

My body tensed. Nothing was there. At least, I saw nothing. But I heard the sound of beating wings coming straight at me.

Had the creature turned into a bat? I couldn't see, but what else would be flying around our house in the middle of the night?

I threw my arms into the air as it came at me. The flying creature veered away from me and then out the doorway.

The creature had left, but it was too late for me to stop my next move.

I toppled backward on my crutches. I felt myself tipping toward the floor. The fall took only a second and most of the sound was deadened by the thick carpet of the dining room floor.

Mentally checking myself for more broken bones, I was pleased not to find any.

Then I heard Aunt Bergen speaking to someone upstairs. It was hard to hear, but I was sure she said, "Elvira, there you are. I am glad you came. Were you out looking for dinner? That was bad. You can have as much as you want from downstairs later. Until then, I have a sweet treat for you in my room."

It was the flying creature. She was named Elvira. I needed to get back to the bedroom before Elvira decided that the sweet treat was not enough for her midnight snack.

I grabbed for a chair, but instead of pulling myself up with it, I pulled the chair over on me with a loud crash.

I pushed the chair off and tried again.

I stretched out my arm to grab the table when something gripped my hand.

# 28

The moment the hand curled its bony fingers around my arm, I screamed and jerked it away.

The creature was not going to get me that easily. I turned my body to face this newest threat when it spoke to me. "I'm sorry. Did I do it once again?"

"Aunt Bergen!" I said with a mixture of surprise, joy, and fear.

"I heard a loud crash down here and hoped that it was not one of my little friends doing some kind of mischief. I can see that it was not," she said as she smiled down at me.

Aunt Bergen helped me to my feet. I told her, "Thanks. I didn't mean to wake you up."

"Oh, I wasn't sleeping. I had to take care of some last-minute things before my big surprise for your family on Christmas. But it's late. We'd better get to bed. Tomorrow is going to be a big day, and I must have my rest," she told me.

I told her goodnight and headed to bed. At that

point, only Glen, Eddie, and I knew her secret. I had to warn them in the morning. I needed some sleep so I could be alert as I struggled against the strange threats in my house.

The moment my head hit the pillow, I was out.

My sleep was interrupted the next morning by hammering outside. The workers had returned to our yard and resumed their building. What are they building? Where's my buddy Glen?" I thought aloud. My question was answered quickly. The phone rang.

"Hi, Conner. This is Glen and Eddie's mom. Have you seen them? Did they stop over there?" she asked.

"No, I haven't seen them yet today. When did they leave?" I asked. I was concerned too.

"Early. They said that they needed to pick up a few things for your Aunt Bergen. They went over there very early, but they never told us where they were going after that," she said.

Oh, no! Aunt Bergen had Glen and Eddie!

**29**

"When I see them, I'll tell them to head home right away," I told her. I was afraid of what might have happened to Glen and Eddie. They might have met the same fate as the moaner in the basement. Aunt Bergen knew that we were onto her plan.

"And, Conner, that is quite a thing the workers are building in your front yard. I can't wait to see your family's reaction. I'll bet your mom is tickled when she sees it," Glen and Eddie's mom said. She chuckled a good-bye and hung up.

How could she laugh at a time like this? She must not have known her own children were missing while on an errand for my alien aunt.

I got out of bed and washed my face. The house was pretty quiet. I could hear Aunt Bergen humming a Christmas carol.

After I dressed, I hobbled to the hallway and out to the kitchen. Aunt Bergen had a strange smile on her face. Then she took a step to the right and revealed behind her a stack of pancakes covered in syrup.

"I thought I'd make you a very special breakfast. I hope you like syrup," she said, placing a bottle near my plate.

"Well, thanks, Aunt Bergen. I really appreciate it. I'm sorry about last night," I told her.

The way that Glen and Eddie's mom talked made me believe that maybe she had been taken over by other aliens in our neighborhood. I remembered seeing a movie about that kind of thing.

Was I living in a very real horror movie?

Aunt Bergen strolled across the kitchen floor and grabbed a basket of clean, folded clothes and headed toward the steps. She called back to me as she climbed upward, "I'm going to put these clothes away and clean up my room. If the workers who are building in the front yard come to the door, let them in. If they have any questions, you can go ahead and answer them."

I rotated my cast-covered leg under the table and sat down so I could eat my pancakes.

The pancakes tasted good. I got a few mouthfuls down before I heard the moaning from deep in the basement. The sound was different. I could tell it was coming from Dad's basement office.

Maybe it was Glen and Eddie! Maybe they were still alive!

I was scared, but then again, I had nothing to lose and my friends had everything to lose if I didn't get down there and help them. Aunt Bergen was going to get me no matter what, but maybe I could save Glen and Eddie.

I scooted toward the basement door. I listened to see if Aunt Bergen was descending the staircase. She wasn't. All was silent except for the moaning.

I was finally going to get to the basement and see who or what was moaning. I pulled open the door.

The kitchen light filled the stairway, and I started moving my feet down. The cast slid down it first. I was ready to make the next step. My hand was on the railing to balance me.

Suddenly, something grabbed me. I lost my balance and tipped forward.

I was about to end it all myself on the basement steps.

# 30

"I'm sorry, kid," the voice boomed at me. A big hairy hand pulled me up from behind before I fell down the stairs. "I knocked on the door, but no one answered. I came back here to see if I could rouse anybody. Where can I find some strong rope?"

It was the worker from outside.

"Thanks for grabbing me before I fell," I told him. "The rope is—" I stopped midsentence.

*Why is he looking for rope?*

"We usually keep rope in the garage, but I don't think we have any now." I tried to act cool and collected.

"By the way, what are you making out there?" I asked.

I wanted him to think that I really didn't care to hear in hopes that he would slip up and tell me.

"Your aunt told me that you would try to get me to tell you. It is going to be a surprise. My kids would die if I had one of these things in the yard. If we had one, they would hang around our house all the time," he said.

"Yes, I guess so," I told him.

As soon as he walked out the door, I hobbled to the window next to the door. I wanted to see what was in the yard.

I laid my nose and eye on the cold glass and tried to see out. It was frosty. I rubbed it hard to remove the thin ice.

Pushing my eye up to the hole again, I saw another eye looking back at me. One of the elves was sitting on the other side of the glass just waiting for me. He gave me a little wave and winked at me—just like Boris had. The elf was probably an alien too.

I felt trapped. What should be the peaceful Christmas season had turned into the season of fright.

I needed to escape, but I didn't know how.

I needed to find Glen and Eddie and rescue them, but I didn't know what to do for them either. I didn't even know where they were exactly.

No, there was no way to get free from the house and Aunt Bergen. I didn't know what Aunt Bergen was, and I wasn't sure that I wanted to find out.

The house had only three outside doors. She had them all covered by her little friends. If I couldn't get out, I needed to find a place to hide. I couldn't go upstairs because Aunt Bergen was up there. I couldn't go down to the basement because the moaner was there—and I didn't know whether the moaner was another victim or the enemy.

Where? Where could I go?

Maybe I could go up the chimney like Santa Claus was supposed to do. Unfortunately, Aunt Bergen had wisely cut off that escape route with her fake Santa Claus legs.

The only hiding place left was in my parents' bedroom. I scooted my weary body there. I lay down on the floor next to the bed. I slid my crutches under it first and then eased my body into the dark and dusty area underneath the bed.

I slid under a few inches. I pulled my broken leg and cast in behind me. I wasn't far enough in. Aunt Bergen would have been able to see me for sure. I slid in a little farther. Still not far enough. I went in farther.

I touched something.

A shoe? Mom or Dad must have kicked a shoe underneath the bed. Then I recognized the feel of canvas and rubber and realized it was actually a sneaker that I was touching.

I pulled on the sneaker. It felt like it was attached to something.

I pulled again.

Whatever it was attached to came with it. I rotated

my head to see what it was. It wasn't one of Mom's or Dad's sneakers.

It was Boris's sneaker.

And Boris was still wearing it.

He had a gigantic grin on his face.

My body was out from under the bed in a flash.

I held back a scream.

I jumped up and grabbed my crutches. I hopped and jumped and hopped again until I was out of the room.

I was scared.

Aunt Bergen was letting me know that she was watching me. No matter where I went, she was watching.

What else had Aunt Bergen done to the house? I left the bedroom and headed for the living room. More decorations that were new to me filled the room. More unusual decorations were hanging on the tree. One of them in particular caught my eye.

I touched it and pushed a little red button on its side. The decoration opened up. Inside was a tiny little choir singing Christmas carols. I thought it was neat until I looked a little closer.

The singers were real. It was like a tiny choir of people inside an ornament.

I was so scared that I hopped backward, forgetting briefly that I was in a cast.

My body tumbled. I went headlong into the biggest stack of gifts I had ever seen. They fell all over me. Some were pretty heavy and hurt as they struck my already bruised body.

I struggled to get up. Every time I moved, more and more brightly wrapped packages tumbled down around me. When the gifts stopped falling, I staggered to my feet.

Something attacked me. It hit my back from out of nowhere. I shouted, "Get off me!"

My arms swung around trying to strike out at it. When I reached over my back, I could feel its fur. *Fur?* I grabbed it and ripped the thing from behind me.

My attacker turned out to be a stuffed reindeer toy that Aunt Bergen must have hung from the ceiling.

But she hadn't done a good job since it had fallen on me. Or had she? Maybe that had been her plan.

I was about to toss the stuffed animal across the room when I heard a loud sound behind me.

Standing in the archway to the living room was a figure dressed in black with a high, pointed black hood pulled over its head.

I gasped.

**32**

"Are you all right, Conner?" questioned Aunt Bergen's voice from inside the hood.

"I knew you were going to come for me sometime. So, this is it? Now is the time you've chosen. I'm not going down without a fight," I yelled at her.

I grabbed my crutches and hopped quickly through the living room and into the dining room.

Aunt Bergen was slowed down by the gifts all over the floor. She was gaining on me, but I knew I could stay a step ahead.

I needed to get to the phone. I had to call 911 and tell them that an alien posing as a relative dressed in a black cape and hood was chasing me around my house on the morning of Christmas Eve.

The cops probably weren't going to believe me, but I had to take that chance. I made it to the kitchen.

"You're not going to make me disappear, and I'm not going to be carried off by flying aliens," I yelled at her.

Aunt Bergen had the most confused look on her face.

As I rounded the corner back into the living room, the phone came into view. I hopped to it and snatched it from the cradle.

My fingers punched in 9–1—but before I could punch in the last number, the phone was suddenly cut off. Aunt Bergen was too far away to have done it.

A hand reached around my head and ripped the phone away from me.

**33**

I turned. I couldn't believe my eyes.

"What were you doing, Conner?" Mom asked.

"Mom! Dad! You're home! Boy, am I glad you made it back before Aunt Bergen did me in. She's got aliens with wings and there's some creature in a box in the basement. Don't you hear the moaning?" All the words spilled out.

"What are you talking about? There's no creature in the basement," Dad said with a puzzled look on his face.

"I know there are. What is the matter with all of you? Are you under Aunt Bergen's spell too? Or was this all part of the plan? Did you plan to leave me here so that Mom's great-aunt would take care of me?"

I was upset. I couldn't believe that my own family was willing to let this happen to me.

"What in the world are you talking about?" Mom asked. "Aunt Bergen, has he been like this the whole time?"

"I don't understand. I thought Conner and I were having a splendid time. I was going to use him in my act tomorrow afternoon," she told my family.

Aunt Bergen stretched out her hand toward me and said, "Come with me, dear. I'll show you what's in the basement and what the workers have been building in the front yard."

"It's all very nice," my dad said.

"Conner, she's just up to her old tricks." Mom was trying to be encouraging.

I was sure that Aunt Bergen, the alien, had somehow gotten to them. I wasn't sure what she could have done to them, but she did it.

"Calm down and tell me what you think is happening," Mom said.

"Aunt Bergen has some kind of beast in the garage and someone—or something—that moans in our basement.

"A dummy named Boris talks and walks and hides in places so he can jump me.

"There are Christmas tree ornaments with living people inside them.

"She has a creature named Elvira living in her room that can fly around the house.

"She's done something with my friends Glen and Eddie.

"If Aunt Bergen is not an alien, this is a nightmare that has come to life.

"And I had to live in the middle of it while all of you were out on the ski slopes enjoying yourselves." I barreled to a stop.

Mom looked at Aunt Bergen. Aunt Bergen looked at Dad. At the same time, they all broke into laughter. Aunt Bergen took a step toward me.

Her hand touched me. I was sure it was the end. "Conner," she said, "I'm sorry for scaring you. I want you to know that I am not an alien."

Mom looked at Dad, and he pulled his arm out from behind him. Something was wiggling in his hands. It was a puppy. The dog's little black eyes were peeking out of long gray fur covering its face.

"You said that you wanted a dog for Christmas. We bought her just before we left. Aunt Bergen was trying to hide her from you so that it would be a surprise," Dad told me.

He added, "That's your basement moaner."

"But what about Boris? And what about Glen and Eddie? You have them caged up in the basement somewhere. What about the creature that flew all over the house and attacked me?" I challenged anybody to answer me.

"We better sit down. I think it's time for me to tell my story," Aunt Bergen said.

Aunt Bergen's face was starting to beam. "Many years ago Uncle Charlie and I did magic shows around the United States. We did shows everywhere.

"Uncle Charlie's favorite illusion was the beast-in-the-box," she continued. "He built the box complete with claws and sound effects so that it seemed like a beast was trying to get out. Then all of a sudden he would pop the box open. Kids thought he made the beast disappear."

*Well, that takes care of the beast in the garage.* "What about Boris?" I asked.

"Boris is my dummy. I once used him in the magic shows. Later, I did church and club meetings with him. I'm afraid that I've gotten out of practice, and I'm sure that you saw me working on my routine. I was hoping to keep Boris as a surprise for the family," Aunt Bergen explained.

"Then explain where Glen and Eddie are. Their mother said that they came over here first," I challenged again.

"Glen and Eddie are such nice kids. Since you're in a cast, I asked them if they would run down to the grocery store to get me things I needed to make dinner tonight. They are probably at home right now.

"By the way, I told them about the magic act and said that I would do an outdoor show for the neighborhood kids in a few days."

114

"You have been able to explain just about everything but the flying creature—and the tree ornaments with living people inside," I said.

"Oh, yes. Every magician uses a dove. That is what I picked up at the bus station. That was why I had to hurry to get Elvira.

"After I got home with her, Elvira got out of the cage and out of the room. She must have come downstairs and perched in the dining room."

I smiled. "Well, you can tell her that I saved her life."

Aunt Bergen looked at me, puzzled. "Why?"

"She was on Mom's antique rocker, and I chased her away before she did anything wrong," I joked.

I was slowly beginning to understand. Aunt Bergen wasn't an alien. She might be a little strange, but she wasn't from outer space.

Aunt Bergen continued explaining. "And the Christmas tree ornaments are small holograms— like the comb I was wearing in my hair when I first arrived. The holograms are made in such a way that the faces inside appear in three dimensions and look as if they are moving. That is my son's new business. He made the ornaments for your family as special gifts."

I turned to Mom and Dad. "But why did Aunt Bergen bring all this stuff to our house?" I asked.

"That's a good question," Mom said.

Aunt Bergen grinned broadly and spoke to us all. "Conner, you of all people should know why."

"I don't know," I said. "But I would really like to know."

"You said that Christmas had become a holiday about presents, and I said the best presents were the ones you gave of yourself. Do you remember?" she asked me.

"I'm afraid that I've been spending most of my time thinking that you were going to take over me and my family," I answered.

Everyone laughed.

"The meaning of Christmas is giving. In the first Christmas, God gave of himself. He gave us the Christ child, the best gift of all. I brought all my things to your house because my Christmas gift to the Morgan family is myself. The magic tricks and Boris are the gifts that I wanted to give to all of you because they are a part of me." She smiled again.

"And the 'elves' you saw are my dear friends and part of my old traveling show. They dropped by to help me get my act ready for you and your family."

I stood up and smiled. I was glad to finally know what was going on. My *first* instincts about Aunt Bergen were the right ones. I did like her. And I was glad she helped me remember what Christmas was really all about.

I turned around to head for the stairs but stopped before I climbed up them. They had explained everything except what the workers were building in the front yard.

Popping open the front door, I stuck my head out to look. A blast of cold air hit my face. It was a miniature stage—for the show Aunt Bergen was going to put on for the kids in the neighborhood!

Boris was sitting in the chair next to the Christmas tree. I looked over at him, smiled, and said, "Have yourself a merry little Christmas, Boris." I turned my head to shut the door.

Just then, a high, strange voice said, "Have yourself a *scary* little Christmas, Conner."

Read and collect all of
Fred E. Katz's

# SPINE CHILLERS™

Don't miss

# Birthday Cake
# and I Scream

*Turn the page for a spine-chilling preview . .*

In a few days I was going to be twelve years old. You would think that a guy's twelfth birthday would be special. I thought so, but the problem was that the "party places" weren't cooperating.

I had planned to take a few of my closest friends to a paintball place. When we called, they already had parties booked for this weekend.

After we found that out, my mom and I called all over town for a fun place to hold my party. I think I heard the same thing a million times. "Sorry, but we're booked that night."

I had completely run out of ideas and hated the thought of uninviting all my friends to my party. I thought that would be the worst thing in the world. At least that was what I thought until Mom gave me what she called "good news."

When I came in from school, I tossed my backpack on the floor by the stairs and headed to the kitchen.

After a long day at school and soccer practice, I needed to refuel. Chocolate chip cookies and a big glass of milk were the fuel of my choice.

I was pouring a tall glass of cow juice when Mom walked in the kitchen from work. She hadn't even put down her briefcase before excitedly telling me, "Kiddo (she always called me 'Kiddo,' but you can call me Mac—MacKenzie Richard Griffin's the name) I have good news for the birthday boy."

"You decided to get me a four-wheeler for my birthday?" I jokingly asked.

"No, it's even better. I found a place for your party."

My face lit up, and my feet felt like dancing. "Where?"

"Spooky the Clown's Halls of Pizza." She beamed as she said it.

My face went gray, and my dancing feet turned to heavy lead sloshing through Jell-O. "Mom, we can't go there!"

She had a puzzled look on her face and asked, "Why?"

"It's for little kids," I protested. "I'll be the laughingstock of the school and the youth group."

"Don't worry. You and your friends will have the entire Halls of Pizza all to yourselves." Mom smiled. "And Spooky the Clown told me that they have an entire room filled with the latest video games. They even have your favorite, Guardians."

"Guardians? They've got Guardians! Hardly anyone has that one."

Mom had a point. If we had the place to ourselves, we wouldn't be bothered by little kids. But I wasn't convinced. "What about the important stuff like—"

"Like pizza? You'll have all the pizza that you can eat," Mom interrupted. "Speaking of eating, if any of us want to eat tonight, I better get something made." Mom grabbed her briefcase and headed to her bedroom to change.

I sat at the kitchen table thinking over my glass of milk and three chocolate chip cookies. I might be convinced that Spooky's place could be a lot of fun, but I wasn't sure that my friends would be.

I felt uneasy, so I decided to wait until lunchtime the next day to tell them. They were all planning to be at my party on Friday night, but would they change their minds about coming when I told them that it was going to be at a little kids' place?

My morning classes went fast. As much as I liked lunchtime, it wasn't going to be my favorite lunch of the year. I was lost in thought as to how I was going to tell them when I heard Frankie call out, "Hey, this way."

I snapped my head up and noticed that I had been walking right past our table. I gave her and my oldest, best friend, Barry, an embarrassed smile.

"Earth to MacKenzie, earth to MacKenzie," Barry

said, imitating the scratchy sound of an old science fiction movie. "Please land at your earliest convenience."

I turned to sit down, and I nearly plopped my body down on another friend, Lisa. She had slipped into the seat as I was snapping out of my what-do-I-tell-my-friends trance. "Sorry, Lisa. I didn't see you come up behind me."

Lisa smiled back at me as I slipped into another chair next to her. I was with my three best friends and I dreaded what I had to say.

Barry Lennon had seen most of my twelve years with me. He lived in the house right behind ours and was in the same Bible class at church. Our parents had tried to grow a nice row of hedges back there on the property line, but Barry and I crushed them down with all our walking back and forth between houses. His mom finally put a gate in the backyard hedges.

Frankie and Lisa were cousins and went to church with us too. Lisa was often at Frankie's house only a few blocks from my house. Since both of them had the last name Grey, we had sat next to each other in our alphabetical elementary school rows ever since first grade. Frankie and Lisa were the neatest girls I knew.

The three of us were on the same ball teams and went to the same youth group. I guess a person could say that we were inseparable. I hated to tell them my news about Spooky's.

"I have some bad news," I told them as a warning. I definitely had their attention and was ready to drop the news about Spooky's onto the table.

I had just opened my mouth when Davis Wong scooted into the seat at the end of the table and asked, "So, when do I get my paintball gun, and who wants to get hit first?"

Davis was the most recent addition to our little group. He had just started at the school this year because his dad was the new vice principal. We first met him at the youth group in the summer. He was a pretty cool kid, but I was finding out that he had a crazy sense of humor.

I didn't know what to do. I suddenly got nervous and blurted out, "The paintball place is booked."

"What?" Frankie cried out.

"No paintball?" Davis's mouth drooped into a gigantic frown.

"I hope you're kidding," Barry stated.

"No, I'm afraid that I'm not kidding. We tried everywhere. It seems that this was a very popular weekend to be born on. All the places have parties going on Friday night," I reported sorrowfully.

"So, what are you going to do?" Frankie asked with genuine concern.

"We got Spooky the Clown's Halls of Pizza," I answered.

Frankie asked, "Isn't that the new place in that old building on Tremble Avenue?"

"Yes, that's it," I responded.

Lisa gasped and got a dead serious look on her face. Then she jumped out of her seat and said loudly, "No, not Spooky's. Anyplace but Spooky the Clown's Halls of Pizza."

"I figured that some of you may not want to go because it's a little kids' place," I told them. My body slumped lower and lower into the chair.

Lisa shot back, "No, that's not it at all. It has nothing to do with little kids. Spooky the Clown's Halls of Pizza is haunted!"

"Come on, Lisa, you don't really believe that old ghost story?" Frankie asked.

"I've heard that people have seen some pretty strange things in that old building," her cousin said defensively.

"What does the ghost do, jump out of pizzas at kids?" Davis joked.

"Don't joke, Davis. There is something unusual about that building. Nothing stays in business very long there," Barry said.

"Remember, last year the restaurant was called something else. And the year before that it was Uncle Andy's House of Sandwiches. When we were little kids, it was the Chunks of Cheese Pizza Parlor. I can't remember all the other names."

Davis had a puzzled look on his face. He asked, "Why do you think that so many places go out of business in that building?"

"It's plain and simple," Lisa stated sharply. "The building is haunted by ghosts, and they scare away customers."

In all my planning for my birthday party I had not stopped to consider that Spooky's was located in the old Tremble Avenue building.

When my friends and I were little kids, the older kids used to tell us stories about the place. They scared us with their talk about ghosts. But that was years ago. We were the older kids now.

Surely Lisa and Barry didn't still believe those crazy stories. Besides, we'd given our lives to Christ. Believing in ghosts and Jesus at the same time just didn't fit.

"Do you think the ghosts are still there? Do you think they will make a special appearance at Mac's party?" Barry asked us.

The bell rang before anyone could respond to Barry's question. As I walked down the hallway to my next class, I remembered those ghost stories the older kids used to tell us. There were nights when I had to keep a night-light on in my room because I was so scared. Just thinking about the stories sent a shiver up my spine.

Get a grip on reality, Mac, I told myself. You've given your life to the Lord, and you're too old to believe in ghosts anyway.

After lunchtime, the rest of the school day seemed

routine. In fact, it was boring. Even soccer practice was boring. We did the same drills over and over again.

I was glad to get out of there because I was supposed to meet Frankie and Lisa at the town library. We were working on a history report together. I chose them as study partners because they were the two smartest students in the class.

When I got to the library, they had already started on the report. "Sorry, the practice went long. How's the report coming?" I asked.

"Not too bad. We've found a lot on the Civil War. Our big problem is narrowing it down to one main topic," Lisa said.

"Maybe I can help," I offered.

"We were hoping you might contribute something to this team. Sit down and dig through these books," Frankie suggested.

Before I sat I said, "I saw a book on the Civil War last week that had some unusual stories in it. It's on the third floor. Let me grab that and I'll be back in a second."

The book was way back in the corner. I had seen it when I was looking for another book. I remembered that it had personal stories from people who had been involved in the war. Some quotes from them could make our report stand out.

People rarely went up to the third floor. I remembered that the book was on the shelf in the farthest corner.

I passed the other old books with their musty smell until I got back in the corner. The light was poor there. Most of it came from a single lamp on a study table at the other end of the row.

After all our talk about ghosts, I was feeling a little frightened. My fear made me move very slowly down the aisle.

Finding the book wasn't going to be as easy as I thought. I kept looking, but it wasn't where I remembered it was. I was kneeling, trying to focus on the book spines in the dim light.

Suddenly, the light was cut off. A large shadow was cast down the aisle. What did it? I looked up, but the figure was gone.

It must have been nothing out of the ordinary. Just someone else looking down the aisle. I went back to my search.

Then the light cut out again. I looked up, and I saw a dark form move away again. It did not look like a person. It spread out, as if it had wings, across the aisle opening.

I found the book and reached for it.

The light was cut off again. I spun my head quickly and caught sight of the form. It was tall and wide.

Two small arms stuck out each side. I could see nothing else. That area of the library was too dark.

Gripping my book, I stood up and backed against the wall. My shadowy, uninvited guest moved down the row of bookshelves toward me. The shape shivered as it approached. The silhouetted ghoul's progress was slow, and my fear grew with each step it took.

I scanned the shelves. I wondered if I could climb them and get away. If I tossed books at the ghoul would it run?

The form took two more steps and stopped. I placed a foot on one of the shelves to prepare myself for an escape. The shelf bent and nearly fell off. That escape route was out of the question.

I grabbed the heaviest books I could find and waited. If the ghoul took another step, I was going to clobber it. I heard it taking heavy, deep breaths. I wondered if it could hear my heart beating like a conga drum.

In the next instant, the dark, shadowy figure leaped for me.

I screamed and tossed a thick, heavy book at the shape. I hit it right in the midsection. The ghoul dropped to the floor, and the library light broke into my corner. In the next second, I saw what was behind the attack.

"That was just a little birthday scare for you," Frankie said through her snorts of laughter. They had carried Lisa's black raincoat with long rulers through the arms. The coat looked spooky.

"Hey, that wasn't funny at all. A guy gets really tense back in a dark corner like that. If I would had hit you with the big book I threw, it might have hurt," I chastised them both.

Lisa reached down and picked up the heavy book. She looked at the cover, and her eyes grew wide. "Very appropriate, MacKenzie. Did you choose this book on purpose?"

"No, I just grabbed a fat one. What is it?" I asked.

Frankie took the book from Lisa. She turned the

spine my way. The book was titled *Our Town's Ghosts and Ghouls*. It was subtitled *And Their Favorite Haunts*.

Frankie tossed it my way. "Are you sure you didn't choose that on purpose?"

"No. I just grabbed a thick one nearby. I couldn't even see the spines of the books. Remember, you cut off all my light," I replied.

"Then this whole thing is spooking me. Is there anything in there about the building on Tremble Avenue?" Lisa asked.

I opened the book to the contents page. I scanned the contents and stopped when I reached the thirteenth chapter. The title under the number read, "The Haunting on Tremble Avenue." I closed my eyes and opened them again. I was trying hard to disbelieve what I had just read. Maybe if I closed my eyes, the words would change.

My heart increased its beat again, and I felt all the moisture leaving my mouth. I managed to mumble, "You're not going to believe this." Lisa looked at me curiously and I handed her the book.

"Look under chapter thirteen." My voice was barely a squeak.

Lisa gasped.

"What is it?" Frankie asked, concern registering in her voice.

Lisa didn't answer. She flipped frantically through

the pages of the book. When she stopped, she began to read.

"The legend surrounding the building at 1313 Tremble Avenue is traced back to the turn of the century. At that time Bertrand Bailey Cooley died mysteriously in the room he rented in the building's basement."

Lisa glanced up at me, then turned her eyes back to the book. She moistened her lips and continued reading.

"Rumor has it that Cooley stashed a fortune somewhere inside the building. The means by which Cooley gained such a fortune are uncertain, considering his employment."

Frankie and I were riveted. We stared at Lisa as she turned the page.

"Cooley worked in the building's first-floor restaurant during the winter season. The rest of the year he was employed as a clown in a traveling carnival."

Lisa abruptly stopped reading and looked wide-eyed at Frankie and me. "A clown!" Her intonation was shrill, though she kept her voice low in the library. "And now a clown is running the restaurant! Don't you think that's more than a coincidence?"

"You can't be serious," Frankie said. "The guy you're reading about died almost a hundred years ago. No. It's just a coincidence, Lisa. Keep reading."

I remained silent. I knew Frankie was right. A

clown who died almost a hundred years ago couldn't be linked to a clown who was alive and running a business today. But still, the thought was unsettling.

"Six months after Cooley's death, another man, Oscar R. Newcombe, died mysteriously inside the Tremble Avenue building," Lisa continued. "Newcombe, the manager of the carnival for which Cooley had worked, was allegedly in search of Cooley's hidden fortune. Newcombe claimed Cooley had stolen the money from the carnival.

"No facts were ever substantiated in the incidents, and no fortune has ever been found. Yet legend has it that the ghosts of Cooley and Newcombe roam the building, frightening anyone who threatens to find the hidden fortune."

I gulped. The fears I had as a little kid hearing the older kids tell me ghost stories about the Tremble Avenue building came rushing back. Fortunately, Frankie was still the voice of reason.

"Eerie legend," she said. "But that's all it is. A legend. There's no such thing as ghosts."

"Don't be so sure," Lisa answered. "The next section of the chapter is subtitled 'Reports of Apparitions and Unexplainable Phenomena.'"

"Hey, we better get to work on our report," I said. I didn't want to hear any more about ghosts, but I didn't want to tell Frankie and Lisa that I was getting spooked.

"Why don't you take this home with you?" Lisa

said, handing me the book. "You can read the rest of the chapter later."

I put the creepy book under my arm and grabbed the one I had come for. We managed to get some work done, though I had trouble staying focused. I wanted to get home soon. The sun was already going down, and in my current state of mind I didn't want to walk home in the dark.

The girls were going to Frankie's house a few blocks away from my home. We walked the several blocks from the library together talking about school, ghosts, the youth group, ghosts, other friends, and ghosts again.

I was still concerned that my friends wouldn't come to my party because they thought that Spooky's was for little kids. I wanted to make sure about Frankie and Lisa.

"Are you two still coming to my party Friday night?" I looked down at the sidewalk. "I mean, even though we can't have it at the paintball place?"

"Of course we'll be there," Frankie said. "You're our friend, Mac."

I looked up at Frankie. She was smiling.

"It will be a private party," I said in an attempt to play up the positive side. "Mom rented the entire place for the night."

"Aren't you two scared of that building after what we read earlier?" Lisa questioned.

"I don't see how a pizza place for little kids could

be haunted. Isn't there some kind of law against that?" Frankie questioned.

I joked, "It's in the Ghosts and Ghouls Handbook."

We rounded the street corner, and the two entered Frankie's house while I continued to my house.

We lived on a dead-end street that was very quiet. Mom and Dad liked that, but sometimes it was a little eerie because of the giant trees that lining both sides of the road. They blocked the streetlights and cast long shadows on the sides of houses. Four of those trees were in our deep front yard. By the time a person got to the front porch, the streetlights had all but disappeared.

After I pushed through the gate in the front yard, I started up the walk. I thought I saw something move around the side of the house. If we had a dog or a cat, I might have thought it was our pet. But all I have is a goldfish, and it doesn't usually go out at night for walks.

I kept walking toward the house. I was a little unnerved, but I figured my eyes were playing tricks on me.

When I was halfway up the walk, I heard a crash in the backyard. At least, it sounded like a crash. Mom or Dad could have been dropping the trash into the garbage can. It could have been something that simple and that logical.

I tried to tell myself that, but I knew it was not

the sound of the garbage can and I knew it scared me. I started singing a Petra tune to bolster my courage.

My shaky legs reached the porch, and I caught myself breathing a sigh of relief. As I let out the air from my lungs, something touched me from behind.

# SPINE CHILLERS™

It's MacKenzie's twelfth birthday, and unlimited
play on the video games makes the party
pretty cool for him and his friends until
Spookie the Clown shows up with
some games of his own . . .

It's too late to refuse the invitation in . . .

# Birthday Cake and
# I Scream

## SpineChillers™ #7
### by Fred E. Katz